The Betrayers

ALSO BY DAVID BEZMOZGIS

The Free World

Natasha

The Betrayers

A NOVEL

DAVID BEZMOZGIS

HarperCollins*Publishers*Ltd

HarperCollins Publishers Ltd
2 Bloor Street East, 20th Floor
Toronto, Ontario, Canada
M4W 1A8

www.harpercollins.ca

ISBN 978-1-44340-977-3

Book design by Carin Dow

Printed and bound in the United States
RRD 9 8 7 6 5 4 3 2 1

To Mae, Lena, and Eve

And when Hadad heard in Egypt that David slept with his fathers, and that Joab the captain of the host was dead, Hadad said to Pharaoh: "Let me depart, that I may go to mine own country." Then Pharaoh said unto him: "But what hast thou lacked with me, that, behold, thou seekest to go to thine own country?" And he answered: "Nothing; howbeit let me depart in any wise."

—FIRST KINGS 11:21–22

There can be no struggle for national liberation without sacrifices and repression, death in battle and the execution of martyrs. And nothing on earth can withstand the power of self-sacrifice.

—DAVID RAZIEL

Sanctuary

ONE

A thousand kilometers away, while the next great drama of his life was unfolding and God was banging His gavel to shake the Judaean hills, Baruch Kotler sat in the lobby of a Yalta hotel and watched his young mistress berate the hotel clerk—a pretty blond girl, who endured the assault with a stiff, mulish expression. A particularly Russian sort of expression, Kotler thought. The morose, disdainful expression with which the Russians had greeted their various invaders. An expression that denoted an irrational, mortal refusal to capitulate—the pride and bane of the Russian people. That Leora persisted in arguing with the girl proved that she was the product of another culture. In Israel, notoriously obstinate country, argument could be sport, sometimes engaged in for its own sake, sometimes to accomplish something. But this Levantine penchant for argument was of no use in a Crimean hotel at high season. Much had changed, Kotler observed—the very existence of this modern hotel and a few others like it; the vacationers in their Western fashions and their brash, contemptuous, cheerful, money-induced postures; all the visible appurtenances of progress and prosperity—but at the root, where it mattered, there was no change. One had only to look at the Russian girl's face. A people's mentality, this hard nut, mysterious and primitive, resisted change. Yet to espouse such a view was now considered provocative, and it was precisely this sort of provocative thinking that had landed him in his predicament, Kotler thought gravely— but not without a twist of ironic satisfaction.

Leora spun away from the registration desk and strode over to Kotler. He regarded her as she approached, a strong-minded Jewish girl, dark curls flying, black eyes fierce with indignation, her solid, compact figure radiating rebuke. Perhaps someone could think, considering them, that here was a dutiful daughter vacationing with her father. But wasn't that yet another of the changes, the increased number of daughters and fathers who seemed to be vacationing together?

—The cow says they have no record of our reservation, Leora announced. An outright lie. I was tempted to tell her whom she was dealing with.

—I'm sure it would have made a profound impression.

—I wouldn't be so dismissive of your importance.

—Well, there's something I've seldom been accused of, Kotler said.

—I don't find this nearly as amusing as you do.

—All right, Leora, what do you propose we do? Write an open letter, stage a hunger strike?

Each trailing a suitcase, they stepped from the coolness of the marble lobby into the bright glare of the esplanade. In his disguise of white Borsalino hat and dark sunglasses, Kotler blinked out at the tourists who flowed past, the waiters who raced among tables at a café nearby, and the customers who beset the souvenir booths along the stone wall. Beyond which: the sea and the sunbathers on the gray pebble beach. So how much had really changed? Kotler thought. Fifty-three years ago, had the picture been so very different? There'd been no modern hotels, and the offerings at the cafés and souvenir booths hadn't been quite so eclectic, but there had still been plenty to enchant a ten-year-old boy. Kotler recalled the open-air concerts, the hikes with his father in the surrounding hills, the excursions to the Greek ruins and the Italian fortress, and the long, aimless, scorching days at the beach. They had spent an entire month this way, he and his parents, their only such time together. In the scheme of his family's story, this one month assumed a legendary, halcyon quality. They never succeeded in repeating it. The following summer, his mother had a terrible appendicitis scare. The summer after that, his father switched jobs. And after that, Kotler's vaunted musical aspirations interceded. His parents agreed that he shouldn't spend so much time away from his piano lessons. The great Myron Leventhal consented to take him on, and Kotler traveled for the first time to Moscow. And after that, it was too late. There was always something else he preferred to do. When he wasn't preoccupied with his studies, he was preoccupied with friends, with girls, and eventually with politics. In retrospect, given the way their lives unfolded, what a shame it was that they never managed to return to Crimea.

Kotler and Leora paused outside the hotel to adjust to their surroundings and circumstances. Leora gazed at the neighboring hotels.

—There's no point, Kotler said, following her gaze. When I called yesterday, they told me I was getting their last room. It's

August. The town is booked up. Everywhere here we'll get the same answer.

He read in Leora's eyes a tempered defiance and disappointment. Tempered, he understood, out of respect and—it couldn't be denied—concern for him.

—Maybe. But it would take ten minutes to find out.

—I'd sooner not waste the time.

—So what, then? Is that it? Do we just fly back?

—No, we've come this far. It would be senseless to leave.

—Wonderful, Baruch. But where will we stay? In a tent on the beach? Like the nudists in Koktebel?

—There's an idea. I can see the headline and the photo: Baruch Kotler Exposed!

—Yes, and where am I in this photo?

—Beside me. Where else? If this is the way it's going to be, let them gape.

—I feel I've seen enough of those photos.

—Never mind that, Kotler said. Anyhow, we haven't moved in with the nudists just yet.

Off the esplanade, he flagged down a taxi, and the driver helped them stuff their suitcases into the trunk. He took them back to the town's bus station, where, not quite three hours earlier, they had arrived on the bus from Simferopol. The atmosphere then had been hectic: vacationers vying for taxis, and a clutch of locals—mainly apartment brokers with brochures and business cards—clamoring for lodgers. At the time, Kotler had paid them little mind. He'd noticed them only insofar as they reminded him that it was with such people that he and his parents had lodged. They had taken a room with a middle-aged Russian couple who lived also with their married son and his family. They had coexisted peaceably, without conflicts, for the entire month, sharing among them not only the kitchen but also the toilet. Simpler times. And now, since it was nostalgia that had, however convolutedly, brought him back to this place, he had no cause to regret what had happened at the hotel. On the contrary, if what he wanted was to revisit the past, to draw as closely to it as he could, then the Russian girl had done him a favor.

The scene at the bus station was no longer what it had been in the morning. Now there were far fewer people about, only a small number of locals grouped together at the end of the plaza, waiting listlessly, some holding their hand-lettered signs across their knees or down at their sides. They roused slightly at the sight of him, Leora, and their suitcases, but none bothered to approach. He and Leora were, after all, unlikely clients, heading, it would seem, in the wrong direction. A thought struck Kotler, and he told Leora to wait with the bags as he went into the bus station to consult the schedule. A stain of pessimism and defeat adhered to the people waiting outside, implicating them in their own bad fortune. Kotler could not repress the suspicion that if they were lingering, if they had failed to attract lodgers, it was for good reason.

—The next bus from Simferopol isn't due for another three hours, he told Leora when he rejoined her.

—And so …?

—When it comes, I expect more locals will return offering rooms. But that still leaves three hours.

—And those people there?

—Those forlorn-looking people? Somebody should teach them the importance of projecting an image of strength.

—We have three hours. You could give them a seminar.

—Yes, well, perhaps now is not the best time.

—Perhaps not.

—Three hours is long enough to investigate one or two places. If we don't find anything we like, we can return in time for the Simferopol bus and see what else materializes.

While they were speaking, Kotler noticed that some of the people had taken a keener interest in them, as if having picked up the scent. When Kotler and Leora started toward the group, two people separated themselves from the others and stepped forward to meet them. They did not appear to be in league; rather at odds. Both were middle-aged women, and each held a hand-lettered sign advertising accommodations. The one who took the lead was stouter and darker complexioned. Her hair had been cut short and dyed an unnatural shade of burgundy. Her features were regular, the eyes, Kotler noticed, a striking dark blue, and though her skin had thickened with age, he imagined that she had been alluring in her day. The second woman was short, shorter than the first, and appreciably shorter even than the diminutive Kotler. She was sinewy, the twin points of her collarbones jutting from the top of her summer frock. She was younger than the first woman by as much as a decade, her hair longer, wheat-colored, and undyed. Each woman wore a small gold Orthodox cross around her neck. Whereas, ethnically, the first woman was harder to place, the second had the snub features of a Russian peasant. Yes, the old game of deducing ethnicity; in this they were all participants, experts.

—Are you looking for a room? the first woman inquired.

—We are, Kotler replied.

—For how long?

—The week.

—I have it. If you'll come with me, I can show you.

—Why should he go with you? the second woman protested. I also have a room. And more convenient. Closer to the beach. Let's ask the client what he wants.

—Here is the difference between my room and hers, the first woman said. Hers may be closer to the beach by five minutes, but it is smaller and lacks a private bath. So it depends what you want. In my experience, people today prefer to have a private bath.

—And the price? Kotler asked.

—Whatever she offers you, the first woman said, I will match it.

—And the others? Kotler said, regarding those who had remained in place and who, in the shade of the glass-and-concrete hulk of the terminal, followed their conversation with a flat, disconsolate interest.

—You're welcome to talk to them. But none of them will offer you anything better. And besides, do you have the time to see every place? Why not come with me? I believe you will be satisfied. But if not, you can come back and try with someone else.

—As usual, Svetlana, you're very aggressive, the other woman said.

—*Pardon, madame?* Svetlana replied, the French words heavily accented with Russian. Exactly who is being aggressive? You have some nerve to insult me in front of clients.

—It's correct that my room doesn't have a private bath, the second woman said to Kotler and Leora, making a point of ignoring Svetlana. But I wouldn't call it smaller. It is also clean and newly renovated. My husband, a qualified carpenter, did the work himself. And it is much closer both to the beach and the bus station. In the interest of saving time, why not come see it first? To go with her will take you twice as long.

Kotler exchanged a quick look with Leora to ascertain her opinion. What he saw from her was mostly demurral, abstention from the vote.

—Where are you from? Svetlana asked, thrusting herself more completely in front of the other woman.

—America, Kotler said and flashed another glance at Leora.

—Are you Jews? Svetlana asked ingratiatingly, in a tone Kotler had never much liked.

—Do you ask this question of all your clients?

—My husband is Jewish, Svetlana stated, as though it were an article of pride.

—Oh, and what of it? the second woman declared, stepping around Svetlana. Maybe my grandfather was a Jew?

—If you're Jews, Svetlana continued, you will understand what life is like for us here.

—Now you're Jewish too? the second woman scoffed. It's news to me. Well, if you're so Jewish, what are you still doing here? The other Jews, those with any sense, skipped off to Israel at the first opportunity.

—You see what we have to put up with, Svetlana said contemptuously.

—Is your husband from here? Kotler asked casually.

—No, from Kazakhstan, Svetlana said, and added defensively, There are many Jews from Kazakhstan.

—Well, I suppose it's better here than in Kazakhstan, Kotler said.

—If you have to struggle for your daily bread, it makes little difference, Kazakhstan or Crimea.

Kotler turned once more to Leora. He now had no trouble discerning her mind. He could tell that she disapproved of his inclination. She was savvy, disdainful of risk, and far less sentimental than he. Without a doubt, hers was the more prudent course, but he had never been good at stifling the contrarian part of his nature. And he was much too old to undertake a transformation.

—Doesn't it say in the Torah that you should first help your own kind? Svetlana pronounced.

—Does it? Kotler replied, but he had already made his decision. And even this comment didn't cause him to revise it.

He gripped the handle of his suitcase and tipped the bag so that it rested on its little wheels. Reluctantly, Leora did the same.

—Very well, Kotler said to Svetlana, after you.

TWO

To get to the house, they rode in Svetlana's boxy little Lada, not so old and yet seemingly unchanged from Soviet times, its interior smelling cloyingly of rose water. The drive, snaking up into the hills away from the coast, took only a few minutes, long enough for them to formally introduce themselves. Svetlana gave her full name, complete with patronymic, and Kotler and Leora provided their former Russian names, omitting their last names; thus, for the first time since his release from prison, Kotler presented himself as Boris Solomonovich, and for the first time since she was a Moscow kindergarten student, Leora introduced herself as Lena Isaacovna. If only for the purposes of reaching back in time, the use of his old name seemed appropriate. Not until he said it did he realize the extent to which simply identifying himself as Boris evoked a former self. A self very distinct from the man he had resolutely chosen to become. Boris. He might as well have said Borinka, the pet name his parents had used for him. His heart swelled at the ghostly sound of it in his head. And though he recognized that he was in a delicate frame of mind, still he was surprised by how vulnerable, how sentimental he had become. How easily and intensely he could be moved by his own thoughts and recollections.

The house Svetlana brought them to was a single story and, like the neighboring houses, showed signs of deterioration and slapdash repairs. She veered her car sharply onto a pitted driveway and came to a stop in front of flaking, pale green stucco walls. Kotler noted that the roof was of terra-cotta tiles, but a newer addition, affixed to the main body of the house like a crude prosthesis, was covered with slanted corrugated metal. Beside this addition was a small patch of dry grass, the domain of some idle brown hens and a white goose. A stunted peach tree clung to life at the edge of the patch. It was an ordinary village house. A plot of land and its modest yield. A life of shtetl dimensions.

Kotler and Leora followed Svetlana to the house but left their bags in the trunk of the car so as not to give the impression of a fait accompli. At the entrance, they conspired to notice the white plastic mezuzah that had been fastened to the doorjamb. Svetlana, not oblivious, and with a glint of self-satisfaction, brushed the object with her fingertips and then pressed her fingers to her lips.

—Normally, my husband would be here, but Saturdays he takes the trolleybus early to Simferopol to go to synagogue. They don't always have ten men for services, the minyan. Svetlana said, savoring the last word.

Inside the house, she whisked them through the rooms that she occupied with her husband. The front door opened out to a sitting room with a sofa, coffee table, and television. Beyond this stretched a corridor. On the right side of the corridor lay the kitchen, with a wooden table and four matching chairs, a modern refrigerator and stove, and a deep, old-fashioned enamel sink. On the left side of the corridor were three doors, all shut, behind which, Svetlana explained, were the bedroom she shared with her husband, the bedroom their two daughters had shared, and a bathroom. With the exception of the kitchen, which boarders were permitted to use, the rest of the rooms were exclusive to her and her husband. The walls of the corridor were adorned by a number of decorative plates, some of a folk-art variety—presumably local—and others porcelain, featuring historical renderings of foreign cities: Krakow, Prague, Zurich. There was a small wooden plaque with a bronze relief of the Wailing Wall—the kind sold on every street corner in Jerusalem. At the end of the corridor hung a framed portrait of a bride and groom.

—My oldest, Svetlana said, indicating the photo. Now in Simferopol. Her husband prefers to be unemployed there.

—He also attends the synagogue? Kotler asked playfully.

—It's not for him, Svetlana curtly replied.

—And your other daughter?

—She is at the university in Kharkov. She studies economics. A brilliant girl, but this summer she is working in a hairdresser's, Svetlana said and shrugged ruefully.

The corridor came to an end and they faced a door. A small window along the right side of the corridor admitted light. The left side of the corridor opened out to a vestibule. Three steps down was another door, which led to the scraggly yard.

—A private entrance, Svetlana said. You would have a key.

She then unlocked the door to the guest quarters and ushered them into a room of some twenty square meters, hardly extravagant, but tidy and bright. It had everything one expected from such a room: a desk, two chairs, a dresser with a small television upon it, and a double bed with the pillows and blue coverlet precisely arranged. The floor was composed of square white tiles; the walls were also painted white. Above the desk hung a rectangular gilt-framed mirror, and above the bed an amateur watercolor of a seascape, with wheeling gulls and little sailboat. Between the desk and the dresser was the door to the celebrated toilet. Svetlana stood behind them as Kotler and Leora peered inside. They saw a light blue commode with its water tank, a sink of the same color, and the raised platform of the shower protected by a translucent plastic curtain. Like the rest of the quarters, the space was cramped but everything looked clean and in good repair.

—Towels are here, Svetlana said.

Folded over a rod that was screwed to the back of the door were two thin, stiff cotton waffle-print towels, not large enough to wrap around a grown person's waist—masterworks of Soviet fabrication.

With the tour concluded, they returned to the bedroom and inhabited a brief silence. Svetlana looked from Kotler to Leora and then said, So.

—We'll need a few minutes to discuss, Kotler said.

—Very well, Svetlana said.

Her eyes then ranged about the room and momentarily came to rest on the bed. She turned and regarded them both as though trying to communicate something wordlessly. A thing too embarrassing to say out loud.

—And if there are other things you need for the room …

Kotler took this as an allusion to the ambiguity of his and Leora's relations. In other words, the discreet offer of a folding cot.

—Thank you, he said.

Svetlana withdrew to the main house, doing a poor job of concealing her resentments: a resentment that they had not immediately agreed to take the room and a resentment that anticipated their inevitable refusal.

Once she had gone, Kotler sat on the bed, bouncing gently to test the firmness of the mattress.

—This is not a good idea, Baruch. It's not worth it.

—What about your sympathies?

—I don't need to prove my sympathies, and neither do you.

—But that's the problem with sympathies, Kotler said with a smile. One keeps needing to prove them.

—Baruch, to stay here is to ask for trouble. And the whole point of coming here was to evade trouble.

—The point. But not the whole point.

—You know what I mean.

—From that woman, we have nothing to fear.

—And from her husband?

—A Kazakh Jew in a Crimean town?

—A Russian Jew. If there is a Russian Jew in the world who doesn't know who you are, I haven't met him.

—Come, sit by me, Leora.

Kotler patted the spot beside him on the bed. Reluctantly, she did as he asked. Kotler reached for her hands and laid them on his thigh. The gesture was paternal and reassuring, but also undeniably more. Through the fabric of his trousers, Kotler felt the warm, birdlike weight of her hands. They sat quietly together and allowed the moment to take its effect. Slowly, as if submitting to fatigue, Leora rested her head on Kotler's shoulder.

—There, my bunny, Kotler said.

What a picture they made, he thought. This voluptuous, serious, dark-haired girl with her head on the shoulder of a pot-bellied little man still wearing his sunglasses and Borsalino hat. Fodder for comedy. And yet, the girl's fingers slipping between the man's thighs dispelled comedy. In its place, the leap of animal desire.

—Leora, I agree this isn't the rational thing. The rational thing would be to stay with the other woman.

—The peasant.

—The hardy, noble peasant. Who doesn't care for Jews and doesn't read the international press.

—It isn't too late.

—Call it curiosity. Call it instinct. And I am a man who has followed his instincts.

—I thought it was principles.

—In my experience, they're one and the same.

Leora straightened up and looked at him.

—You know my position. What more can I say?

—If you trust me in large matters, trust me in small.

—Baruch, it isn't trust, it's agreement. Usually, I agree with you. I agree with you like with no one else.

—Well, then this time will be an exception. Or more precisely, an evolution. Between two people, trust is more important than agreement. I am asking for your trust. Do you trust me on this?

—I disagree with you, Baruch, but I will not fight with you about it.

—Good. That is the definition of trust.

They found Svetlana in the kitchen, rinsing beet greens in the sink.

—So you have decided? Svetlana asked, not bothering to extract her hands from the sink.

—We will take the room, Kotler said.

—Is that so? Svetlana said, warming not at all.

—We will pay in cash for the week in advance. If that suits you.

—Yes, Svetlana said evenly, that suits me.

THREE

As the sun started its slow midsummer descent, they settled into their room. Svetlana had provided them with keys to the front and back doors and then done them the favor of graciously disappearing. For a moment—after they had finished arranging their belongings in the drawers and cabinets, and after they had stowed their empty suitcases in a corner—Kotler and Leora regarded each other with a mixture of wryness, giddiness, and apprehension. They had stolen away to hotel rooms before, but, except for one instance, never for more than an afternoon or an evening. Six months earlier, on a diplomatic visit to Helsinki, Leora had prevailed upon Kotler to let her stay the night in his bed. But there, she had had her own room a few doors away. Here, for the first time, they had created the semblance of a shared home. Their clothes resided in the same dresser, the same drawers. In the bathroom, huddled together in the shallow cabinet, were their vitamins, pills, creams, and toothbrushes. They were now publicly what they had been privately—which meant they were now altogether something else. Leora still had her apartment in Jerusalem, but as for himself, Kotler thought, this room arguably represented his only home. As matters stood, he had no other.

Liberated from past constraints, free to indulge themselves as they wished—as they had declared they would if only given the chance—neither of them could quell the feelings of restlessness and anxiety. Kotler had been on the run for nearly two days. He'd packed his little suitcase and slipped out of his house before dawn on Friday, hiding out first in his office and later in Leora's apartment. And for much of the day now he and Leora had been traveling, beginning with the surreptitious early-morning flight from Tel Aviv to Kiev, another from Kiev to Simferopol, the bus from there to Yalta, and then the imbroglio with the hotel. All this time they'd barely had a chance to catch their breath and apprise themselves of what was happening in the world. In Kiev, during their layover, they had briefly been able to access the Internet, but it had still been too soon for there to have been any reaction or commentary. Leora had also phoned her father and had the pained, unpleasant conversation. Kotler stood beside her, close enough to overhear part of what her father said and to feel the blot of disapproval. She was her parents' only child, very much her father's daughter, and had lived her life to merit his good opinion. A decade younger than Kotler, Leora's parents had also been Zionists and refuseniks. When their application to emigrate was denied, they'd been trapped in Russia for the final eight years of Soviet rule, though, unlike Kotler, they had been spared the adventure of the Gulag. Yitzhak and Adina Rosenberg—good, intellectual, fair-minded people. Kotler came to know them in Israel at the periodic gatherings of former refuseniks. It was at one of these gatherings that Yitzhak introduced Kotler to his young daughter, a top student at Hebrew University with an interest in politics. When Kotler later hired Leora for his staff, her parents were exceedingly grateful. That was four years ago. Each of those years, they sent a fruit basket to Kotler's house for Rosh Hashanah. Rosh Hashanah was again approaching, but Kotler supposed there would be no fruit basket this year.

To get to the heart of Yalta, he and Leora didn't bother to ask Svetlana for directions but left through the back door, scattering fowl. Kotler led them toward the coast. He flattered himself by thinking that he was navigating from childhood memory, that his sense of the place inhered in him from all those years ago. Closer to the truth was that the town was not very large and sloped downward toward the sea. A few stops on a minibus soon returned them to the tourist center, depositing them near Lenin Square, where, framed heroically by the Crimean Mountains, the bronze Bolshevik still stood on his pedestal looking intently out to sea—and peripherally at a McDonald's. In time, Kotler thought, the good citizens of Yalta might resolve, if not to add a pile of bones at his feet, then at least to replace him.

Without too much trouble, Kotler and Leora located an Internet café, dark as a grotto and occupied mostly by teenage boys wearing headphones and hollering to one another as they shot at Chechens or the Taliban on their computer screens. Kotler had once caught Benzion playing a similar game. A sensitive, studious boy, he was then a student at the yeshiva. Seeing his father's reaction, he'd said shamefacedly, *The guys were playing it.* Now, stationed near Hebron, he was no longer playing.

They found two available terminals next to each other at the back of the café and began with the Israeli press. It didn't take them long to find what they were looking for. The lead stories in both *Haaretz* and the *Jerusalem Post* featured the same photograph of the two of them in the Tel Aviv airport. The photograph captured them as they presented their documents at the ticket counter. It had been taken from a distance, furtively, by another traveler, Kotler presumed, as the professionals never suffered from such scruples. Still, there could be no mistaking their identities, particularly his—though he supposed Leora had now attained a level of notoriety to match his own. *Haaretz* also provided a companion photo of his wife shopping for Shabbat at a market near their Jerusalem home. In the photo, Miriam looked every bit the aggrieved, steadfast spouse, the victim of her husband's treachery. For the article, she said only that she refused to discuss "a private family matter." Kotler could imagine the scene at the market, the pestering, beseeching journalists. But with Miriam they stood no chance. At this thought Kotler permitted himself a fond smile. Miriam was a rock. In her time she had undergone a harsh apprenticeship and was as canny about the press as any image consultant. The reporters could flatter themselves that they had caught her in an unguarded moment, but Kotler would have been surprised—and, frankly, disappointed—if Miriam hadn't orchestrated the whole thing, down to the potato in her hand when they took her picture.

In both newspapers, "the *scandale* Kotler" shared the front page with news of the Knesset's vote in favor of the withdrawal from the settlement bloc. It had gone as predicted, with the prime minister's coalition eking out a narrow majority. Kotler, not wanting to be on record as merely abstaining, had cast his vote the previous day, shortly before his ignominious escape. The *Haaretz* article listed his name among the notable opponents, prominent among the defectors from the prime minister's cabinet. Then there were the obligatory quotes from the various factions. The same choir singing the same song. The prime minister cited defensible borders and the welfare of the Israeli state. The chief of staff spoke of the army's inviolable discipline. The Left rejoiced. The Right seethed. The Americans applauded. The settlers pledged bloody insurrection. And the Palestinians complained.

The din would continue until the operation was executed. What happened then, nobody knew. *Nothing good,* was Kotler's opinion. The only question was just how bad.

He felt Leora's hand on his arm. On her computer screen was displayed a column from an Israeli Russian newspaper. There again was the same grainy photograph from the airport.

—At least here someone bothered to add one plus one, Leora said.

That someone was Chava Margolis, his old friend turned foe, once the mother superior of the Moscow Zionists, the strict, ascetic Krupskaya of their movement. As one of the witnesses against him in his Jerusalem trial, she had later wished to undo him, but here she was saying what any reasonable person should have said: That it was cynical and vindictive of the prime minister to destroy a man's family simply because that man wouldn't bend to his political will. That such an act tarnished the prime minister far more than it did Kotler, particularly as, in the end, it achieved no political goal. And that even people like herself, who had long since grown disenchanted with Kotler, should, instead of gloating over his humiliation, take a moment to reflect upon the reptilian soul of the man who was leading their country. She then added, as professional journalistic practice demanded, that her accusations against the prime minister were speculative, given that no evidence had yet been found to connect him to the incriminating photographs that had been leaked, anonymously, to the press. But she felt that only a child of extraordinary naïveté would believe that the prime minister wasn't involved. And she hadn't met any such children in the entire state of Israel.

Kotler knew that no evidence would ever be found. The prime minister was many things, but he was no amateur. Kotler doubted the press would ever even trace the man who had contacted him. Kotler had known more than his share of security agents and spies, and, as in any walk of life, there were the addle and the adept. But the man he had met, who had introduced himself as Amnon, was a seasoned operator.

Two days earlier, this Amnon had called Kotler on his private cell phone, thus bypassing his staff. How he got the number, Amnon didn't bother to explain. He asked that Kotler meet him that evening in the park behind the Israel Museum to discuss a matter of great consequence not only to the state but also to Kotler's personal life. He instructed Kotler to come alone.

—You should not fear, the man said. There is no threat to your physical safety.

The threat, Kotler was made to understand, was of a different nature.

He rather suspected what the matter was about. For weeks he had criticized the prime minister's decision to unilaterally withdraw from the settlement bloc. At first Kotler had done so strictly *in camera*. They were mostly allies of political expediency, he and the prime minister. Kotler had pledged the eight mandates his Russian immigrant party had won in the previous election to allow the prime minister to patch together his ruling coalition. For this, he had received his ministerial portfolio and, presumably, the stature and influence that went with it. He also had the residual respect afforded to an old Zionist hero, although politics, that indiscriminate blade, eventually cut everyone down to size. So when the prime minister ignored his objections, Kotler voiced his opposition first in the Knesset and then on the op-ed page of the *New York Times,* where he vowed to resign from the cabinet if the prime minister pursued his plan. After that, the usual pressures were brought to bear. His office was inundated with angry phone calls and letters. The prime minister sent his lackeys, first with carrots, then with sticks. All of this was in keeping with what passed for normal political discourse in Israel—at the best of times, no place for gentle souls. But involving a man like Amnon exceeded all bounds.

Still, Kotler agreed, unflinchingly, to the meeting. Not out of curiosity or apprehension, but because he had learned that there was only one way to deal with people like Amnon. You had to stand before them and look them in the eye. Otherwise they started thinking that they could exert power over you.

Kotler went to meet Amnon at eight in the evening, at the very onset of dusk. The trees cast long crisp shadows. A smattering of people filtered through the park—ordinary Jerusalemites glad for a respite from the summer heat, as well as the day's last visitors to the museum. Kotler walked along the footpath, drawing only the occasional glance. His manner betrayed no distress. He, in fact, felt none. He felt, if anything, a familiar sense of contentment. A purposefulness. Fifteen minutes earlier, he had gotten up from his dinner table, kissed his wife and daughter, and calmly walked out the door.

At the appointed place, Kotler saw a burly man in his late forties. His hair was shaved down to dark stubble, sunglasses perched atop his head. He wore a yellow short-sleeved polo shirt whose fabric was stretched by his broad shoulders and thick arms. To complete the image, with his blue jeans he sported a pair of modern athletic sandals, a kind meant for hiking. He looked like certain other sabras of his generation who cultivated the air of retired colonels and regarded the world with the relaxed leer of the habituated military man. In his left hand, held leisurely against his thigh, he had a letter-size manila envelope. As Kotler approached, the man smiled exuberantly and extended his right hand like an old schoolmate or favored cousin. Kotler played along and allowed the man to shepherd him to a vacant bench under a gnarled carob tree.

There they sat in relative privacy, engaging in a conversation that, to a casual observer, would have seemed perfectly congenial. There were no raised voices, no scowls. Not the least sign of agitation. Thus was such business conducted.

Amnon said, I'm here on behalf of an interested party.

—What party might that be? Kotler asked.

—It's of no consequence.

—Is that so?

—Mr. Kotler, you're a politician. You've taken an unpopular position. You must know that many people are unhappy with you. Some of them contacted me. Who specifically? Avi, Yossi, Moshe, Dudi. What does it matter? If I told you who, it would only be a distraction. *Who* isn't important.

—So then.

—So then these people wanted to give you one last chance to change your mind.

—You see? You say *who* isn't important, but it is important. Clearly, if these people knew me at all, they would know that this here is a waste of time. With me, this road leads nowhere. I am a famously stubborn person, Mr. Amnon. Famous for being stubborn. I assume you're aware of this.

—I am, Mr. Kotler. I am a great admirer of your stubbornness. But I assume you are aware that, even without your cooperation, the vote will still go in favor of the withdrawal. In this instance, your stubbornness won't change the outcome.

—So then why bother with me?

—Because the people I represent would like to see everything go as smoothly as possible. They are concerned about the safety of the soldiers and the settlers both. It is an emotional issue. And you are an influential person. People respect you. They listen to what you have to say. If you continue to speak out against the operation, you could incite a bad reaction. You yourself may not be aware of the consequences.

—If the people you represent fear the consequences, they should be the ones to reconsider. We live in a democracy, Mr. Amnon. This is Israel, not Iran. In a democracy a man can speak his mind. When I speak out against this plan, it is not to incite a bad reaction, it is to prevent my country from making a bad mistake.

—That is all very well, Mr. Kotler. But you have had your say. You have had it in the Knesset and in the pages of the *New York Times*. Now you are being asked to be quiet for a little while. You are being asked not to make a big production by resigning from the cabinet. Nobody is even asking you to say you support the operation. You are just being asked to step into the shadows for a moment.

—Mr. Amnon, I will be as clear as I can. I spent thirteen years in Soviet jails and camps fighting for my right to come to Israel. If you or the people you represent think that I can be intimidated by this sort of KGB thuggery, you are mistaken.

—Mr. Kotler, I didn't expect you to say otherwise. In fact, I confess that I would have been disappointed if you had. But since your opposition will not materially change the outcome, I ask why you should martyr yourself in vain?

—Now we're speaking of martyring?

—Believe me, this gives me no pleasure.

—Mr. Amnon, the KGB read from the same script.

—The truth is, I am trying to protect you.

—Line for line.

At this, Amnon let his hand fall upon the envelope that he'd rested in his lap.

—No pleasure at all, he said.

—Let's try without the theatrics, Kotler said.

Amnon smiled ruefully and tapped the envelope with an index finger. He proceeded to slide it from his own lap over to Kotler's. He did so as if with profound regret, as if under duress. Kotler let it lie there without touching it.

—You can feel free to open it, Amnon said.

—I haven't the least interest, Kotler replied.

—Now who is being theatrical?

Kotler picked up the envelope, felt the slickness and pliancy of its contents, and returned it to Amnon.

—They are photographs, Mr. Kotler.

—So they are.

—I encourage you to take a look before you dismiss my proposal.

—Mr. Amnon, I hope I haven't given you the impression that we are engaged in a negotiation. There is nothing in those photographs that would lead me to change my mind. Rest assured, I have a healthy appreciation of my own vulnerabilities. However, if, God forbid, those photos depict some indiscretion committed by my children or my wife, I am sure your people would have, if not the moral, then the political sense not to publicize them. In either case, I have absolutely no desire to look at your garbage.

That was the end of their conversation. Amnon walked off with his garbage and the next morning it was plastered on the front page of every newspaper in Israel.

FOUR

Small round halogen lights had been set into the flagstones of the promenade, evidently part of some recent beautification project. From Lenin Square, the lights formed an illuminated path that extended about a kilometer, as far as the Hotel Oreanda. After a dinner at a restaurant that overlooked the square and the harbor, Kotler and Leora followed the path, leisurely now, feeling, for the first time since the news had broken, not like two culprits harried and pursued. The day's heat had subsided, and the nighttime air felt gentle, consoling, as if bestowed upon them by a sympathetic spirit. The day's throngs had also thinned, and most of the people on the promenade proceeded as they did, without urgency, seemingly without destination. At a certain point, a column of shops and nightclubs split the promenade into two branches. The lower branch bordered the sea; the upper branch ran between two rows of storefronts. For no particular reason, Kotler and Leora followed the upper branch and saw themselves reflected in the darkened storefronts on either side. Out in the open, with their images duplicated again and again, it was as though they had unwittingly made a bold statement of exhibitionism. Not only could they now be seen but, in this hall of mirrors, they could not be missed.

They walked for some time without speaking. With their arms linked, they gave the impression of a couple complete unto themselves, unburdened by the sorts of complications that could lead a person with a constitution weaker than Kotler's— weaker than Leora's, he believed—to commit some desperate, rash, irredeemable act. In the matter of taking one's self in hand, Kotler had world-class credentials. He had mastered his emotions in circumstances far more dire than these. To prove the point to himself, he summoned up an anodyne image from childhood, from this very place, fifty-three summers ago.

—Did I tell you my father was something of a sportsman? Kotler said to Leora.

She shook her head.

—In Lvov, as a boy, before the Soviets took over, he played soccer and ran track and field for the Maccabi sports club. He claimed to have been their best sprinter.

—That's something else you never told me. Your father was Zionist?

—He didn't tell me himself until I informed him that I wanted to immigrate to Israel. I knew growing up that he took a dim view of the Soviet Union, but only in the way most children knew such things about their parents. He'd make a veiled remark. He'd listen covertly to the BBC. But not until I announced myself did he reveal that he had once been the fleetest little Zionist in Lvov!

—No, you never told me, Leora said.

By the time Kotler was a boy, his father was no longer in shape to run. At the front he'd been wounded in the knee, and the wound had never properly healed. Nevertheless, he retained his love for sport and tried to cultivate this interest in Kotler. Physically, they looked very much alike—there were a few childhood photos of his father preserved from before the war, and Kotler could see that the resemblance between him and his father was striking. Even now, when Kotler looked in the mirror, he saw his father's face. Increasingly, he sought his father's face—but that was another story. Yet somehow, in spite of this resemblance, Kotler had failed to inherit his father's knack for running. His father did not easily accept this. When Kotler was little, his father tried to train him. They'd be walking on the street and he'd point to a tree or a lamppost fifty meters away and tell Kotler to run to it. They'd do the whole thing very formally. Kotler would get down into a crouch and his father would keep time on his wristwatch. *Borya: Ready, steady, go!*

Kotler saw a version of this scene before his eyes. The length of pavement near the building they had inhabited in Lvov. He remembered his father calling the commands, and he also remembered hearing neighbors taunt him with the mocking couplet *Zhid, zhid, na verevochki bezhid. Kike, kike, running on a string.* And here in Yalta, perhaps on this very stretch, in the late evening, they had repeated the exercise. *Solomon, stop torturing the boy!* his mother had admonished his father, who had dismissed her with a wave of his hand. Meanwhile, little Borinka knelt down and looked over his shoulder to see his father peering intently at his watch face, the device pinched between the thumb and index finger of his right hand. Kotler knew he wasn't fast, but he wanted to please his father. And, on some level, his childish heart never quite relinquished the hope that, miraculously, the next time, his legs would unleash their latent power and whirl beneath him like a blur.

Kotler released Leora's arm and handed her his hat.

—Time me, he said with an impish smile. From here to that post.

Leora arched an eyebrow, but Kotler was already bending down to assume a semblance of the sprinter's crouch, or as much of one as the constraints of age and inactivity allowed.

—Whom should I call if you have a heart attack?

—An ambulance, Kotler said.

Kotler looked up at her. From here to the post, he said. Ready, steady, go.

Leora shook her head with mild exasperation but turned her wrist and held her watch face between her thumb and index finger, just as his father had.

A few people gazed with benign amusement at the spectacle of the little potbellied Jew chugging along the promenade, knees and elbows pumping. Kotler clapped his palm on the post when he reached it, making a satisfying, declarative noise. Then he trotted back to Leora like a spaniel, beaming with self-satisfaction.

—So, how did I do? Kotler asked.

—A new world record, Leora said. She reached over and gently wiped the perspiration from his brow. How do you feel? she asked.

—Like a boy.

—You are a boy, Baruch. People say you took up with a younger woman, but the truth is that I took up with a boy, Leora said affectionately.

—That's because with you I can be a boy.

On Karl Marx Street they saw a collection of cars waiting, marked taxis on one side and unmarked sedans on the other. The drivers of the unmarked sedans—bored, surly-looking men—leaned against their vehicles. Across the way, the cabbies congregated in a group, smoking and bantering. One of them, a short stocky man with a baseball cap and a yellow reflective vest—the kind worn by crossing guards or construction workers—spoke occasionally into a walkie-talkie and barked orders at arriving drivers.

Because they were already on that side of the street, Kotler and Leora approached the driver of one of the sedans, whose car was at the head of the line. Grim-featured, with a thick black mustache, he looked to be from the Caucasus. As they neared, he eyed them as if he suspected they were out to do him ill.

—You're for hire? Kotler asked genially.

—I am. Where to?

Kotler named the street.

—One hundred hryvnia, the man replied bluntly.

The sum amounted to a little over ten dollars, hardly a fortune, well within their means, but, Kotler felt, inflated nonetheless. He was long in the habit of not letting himself be arbitrarily bettered. In this regard, a man was well advised to be scrupulous. Slacken here or there, let this or that trifle pass, and it set a bad precedent, eroded the substrate of one's character.

—It's a little high, Kotler said.

—If you don't like it, the driver replied, you can go across the street. Ride in one of theirs. But I bought this car. It belongs to me. A Nissan Maxima. I paid for it with my own money. I take care of it. I answer for it. What do you expect me to accept in return, crumbs?

—I understand, Kotler said and took Leora by the arm.

If righteous anger was the man's negotiating tactic, Kotler didn't care for it. He'd encountered it in more consequential settings and hadn't indulged it there either.

—If you understand, then pay! the driver shouted after them.

Kotler and Leora crossed the street to the taxi stand.

—And they ask why we didn't make peace with Arafat, Kotler said.

Since the man with the vest and the cap was the authority, Kotler addressed him.

—Fifty hryvnia, the man said, precluding any need to negotiate.

—Very well, Kotler replied.

He was surprised to see the man walk to the lead cab, shrug out of his vest, and toss it and the walkie-talkie through the driver's-side window and onto the passenger seat. The man then opened the driver's door and climbed inside. How the other cabbies were supposed to manage without his generalship, Kotler didn't quite understand. But wasn't that the beauty of life—when it departed from sense? The little car, another Lada, sputtered to life and Kotler and Leora took their places in the back.

The driver stepped on the accelerator and the car bolted forward. Traffic was sparse but the driver pressed ahead as if he were in a terrific hurry. He weaved around slower vehicles and aggressively took the turns. Kotler and Leora were thrown against each other like riders at a Luna Park.

—We're on vacation, Kotler called to the driver.

—What's that?

—We're on vacation, my friend. We're in no hurry.

—Ah, forgive me. Habit, the driver said and slowed down.

He glanced at them in the rearview mirror as though really seeing them for the first time.

—Where are you from? he asked.

—Moscow, Kotler said, after sifting through his mind for the appropriate choice.

—Moscow? Intellectual people like you? What are you doing here?

—Meaning?

—One doesn't encounter many people from Moscow. Not intellectual people. I thought the fashion was to go west. To Turkey or Cyprus.

—We've been west. We got nostalgic for Crimea.

—I suppose, the driver said. If one hasn't been for a long time. I don't have the right perspective. I'm here every summer now for twelve years. To me, Cyprus sounds good. But for that you need money. Have you been there?

—I have, Kotler said. But only for work.

—You're a businessman? A banker?

—No, nothing like that. International development.

—Oh yeah? the driver said, with due indifference.

Kotler had in fact been part of a UN-sponsored mission to see how deeply the Cypriot Turks and Greeks had buried their hatreds. Deep enough for radishes, Kotler had felt. In a generation or two, maybe deep enough for olives.

—Even after their crisis, I hear Russian people still keep accounts in Cyprus, the driver said.

—Apparently, Kotler said. I personally don't. But Lena here does.

—Is that so? Is it hard to get one?

—The more money the easier, Leora said.

—Isn't that the truth! the driver said mirthfully.

They had turned off the main road and started up into the darker foothills. The driver maneuvered the car along streets that were badly lit and seemingly unmarked. He accomplished this while swiveling his head back to better engage Leora on the subject of her fictitious numbered bank account. After all his illustrious battles, Kotler thought, wouldn't this be a fitting end.

—If I had the money, I'd stash it there. Then I'd go on vacation and pay it a visit. The driver laughed. Now, that's relaxation! A few hours on the beach and then pop into the cool vault to see my money, give it a little cuddle, make sure it's safe and sound. Isn't that how the rich live?

—Once a week, without fail, we go to the bank and cuddle our money, Leora said. Or our health suffers.

—Ha! the driver laughed again and sought Kotler's eyes in the rearview mirror. What a girl! You're a lucky man.

—Evidently, Kotler said.

—Does your missus know? the driver asked.

—Pardon?

—Your missus, the driver repeated affably. Mine is in Donetsk, where I'm from. I'm here only in the summers. To earn money. I have a girl here too. It's natural. My missus knows but she has a modern attitude.

—Well, Kotler said, mine has an ancient one.

At the house, the lights were on in the front rooms. Through the closed windows, the unintelligible sound of a television program surged and plummeted. Holding hands, Kotler and Leora fumbled in the darkness along the side of the still-unfamiliar house. Kotler kept expecting to rouse a goose or a hen but the birds had apparently retired to their roosts. Sensible, reliable, domestic chicken life. Short on excitements but also on dismays.

Kotler found the lock with his key and opened the door. Leora crossed the threshold but Kotler tarried, still holding her hand.

—I should call home, he said. Call Dafna.

A look of apprehension played fleetingly across Leora's face, quickly replaced by her native composure.

—I have to let them know I'm all right.

—Of course.

Leora stepped inside, leaving Kotler to close the door behind her.

He walked away from the house and stood in the middle of the patch of grass. It was the best he could manage under the circumstances. A father calls his young daughter to confess a sin of the flesh: such a call should be placed from the highest mountaintop or bobbing in the middle of the ocean, as a speck on a dark stage, reduced by biblical vastness. A conversation that, God forbid, none but God should overhear.

Three practiced swipes of his finger across the screen—a sequence of tiny movements so routine as to be almost unconscious—and Kotler was looking at Dafna's name and phone number. He tapped the screen, and the little glass rectangle beamed its signal. Thus were such daunting actions undertaken now, with a few twitches of a fingertip. Nothing like the old mindful ceremony of writing a letter, bent at the kitchen table or in the solitude of a prison cell. Not even like the experience of the telephone booth, with the solid, goading, reproachful machine. Still, ceremony or no, the consequences remained the same. You made decisions and, sooner or later, you were called to account.

Kotler listened to the beseeching sound of the ringtone. He knew how the technology worked. At the other end, his name would appear, and Dafna would know who was calling. It was past eleven thirty at night in Yalta, the same time as Jerusalem. Dafna often spoke on the phone with her friends at this hour or later. He and Miriam had occasionally scolded her for it, though not with any conviction. She was a good girl, a conscientious student. By the standards of a modern eighteen-year-old, she could not even be called rebellious. Miriam would have liked her to be more devout, but given that Kotler's own level of religious devotion left a lot to be desired, there was only so much Miriam could legitimately expect. Within a family there were any number of possible configurations, alliances, and affinities—none set in stone, all open for renegotiation unto the grave—but for them, things had assumed a fairly standard alignment: the son took after the mother, the daughter after the father. What enabled Miriam to wholeheartedly embrace God and His strictures, she had passed on to Benzion. And whatever independence, whatever unruliness of spirit Kotler possessed, had been imbibed or inherited by his daughter. Even if angry with him, her way, like his, would be to confront, not to evade.

—Where are you? he heard his daughter say in a parental tone.

—A quiet place, Kotler replied.

—Another secret? Dafna said acerbically. I've been calling you.

—I know, Dafnaleh, Kotler said. I would have liked to call you sooner, but it wasn't possible.

He heard the rustling that implied his daughter was in motion.

—Where are *you?* he asked.

—Home.

More rustling. Then it stopped.

—Is your mother there?

—You didn't call to speak to her, did you?

—No, I called to speak to you.

—Rabbi Gedalia is here. He's with her in the other room. They know I'm talking to you.

—How is she?

—How do you think? You hurt her, Papa. She didn't deserve it.

—You're right. She didn't.

—But you did it anyway.

—Dafna, those are two separate things. The first is not something for a father and daughter to discuss. As for the second, you will have to believe me that I had no choice.

—I don't want to talk with you about sex either, but I'm not a child and I'm not naïve. And don't forget, we live in Jerusalem, the most sex-crazed place in the world, where half the people wear wool sacks to keep from having sex with everyone else. So you didn't wear a wool sack and you surrendered to your desires.

Your desires. The words spoken boldly and neutrally, as if to rise above her disgust at the squalidness of her father's passions.

—I won't even say her name. It makes me sick to think of all the times she was in our house pretending to be loyal and respectful. Pretending to be my friend. She should have had some shame. But it doesn't matter now, does it?

—What do you want me to say, Dafna?

—Are you planning to marry her?

—I don't know my plans. Not about that, not about other things.

—I don't understand. If you don't even know your plans, why did you allow this entire mess to happen?

—As I said, Dafnaleh, I had no choice.

On the other end of the line, his daughter fell silent. A simmering, frustrated silence. Kotler imagined her in her room sitting cross-legged on her bed, glaring at the wall with her dark, intelligent eyes. What could be said about a father's love for his children? You loved them entire. You loved even their anger at you. For what was this anger if not a frustration maddeningly entangled with love?

Kotler waited for Dafna to speak again. She was in her room, in the familiar space. He could imagine her, but she couldn't have imagined him. At that moment he could hardly have imagined himself. In the distance was the bold black silhouette of the Crimean Mountains set against the moonlit sky. There was the quiet road, raked occasionally by the headlights of a passing car. There were the low-slung houses, even in the darkness, haphazard and needy, making their emotional appeal. And in front of him was the bright windowpane, offering a view of the conventional tedium of his landlords' lives. He saw Svetlana rise from her seat and cross the room, carrying a folded newspaper in her hand. She stopped and said something over her shoulder to someone who wasn't visible to Kotler. The Jewish husband, Kotler assumed, returned from his communal duties.

—When you say you had no choice, Dafna finally said, what are you talking about? I don't understand. What exactly didn't you have a choice about?

—Blackmail, Dafnaleh, Kotler said.

—Blackmail?

—I still believe in the policy that one doesn't negotiate with terrorists.

—What did these terrorists want?

—It shouldn't matter what they want. Whatever they want is what you cannot allow them to have.

—But what did they want?

—My silence.

—And what did they promise you for your silence?

—Their silence.

—Their silence? About you and her.

—I didn't bother to ask.

—But that's what it was.

—That's what it turned out to be.

—And you didn't understand that's what they were threatening you with?

—I understood well enough.

—You understood and still you let them do it? Dafna nearly shouted. Didn't you know what it would do to us?

—Yes, Dafna, I knew, but one thing has nothing to do with the other. There are matters of principle where you cannot compromise. Under any circumstances. If I'd compromised, it would have been worse. Far worse for all of us. For our country and for our family, which is part of our country.

—But who cares about the country if it destroys our family? The country doesn't care. All you need to do is read the newspapers to see how the people in this country care about us. To hear the disgusting things they're saying on television. Have you seen the television where you are?

—No.

—Have you called Benzion?

—Not yet.

—He won't say a word about it, but imagine what it's like for him now. Did you think about that? He has to face it all. The army offered him a leave. He should have taken it. I told him to take it. But he wouldn't.

—Dafnaleh, this will pass. You have to believe me. I speak, unfortunately, from great experience.

—I know about your experience, Papa. Everybody knows. You've sacrificed and sacrificed for this country, but they still ridicule you. They ridicule you *because* of your sacrifices. So what good is it? Let somebody else sacrifice for a change. And if nobody else wants to, then who are you sacrificing for?

One sacrificed for one's people as one sacrificed for one's children. One did it because one felt that one knew better than they did. That one saw in them what they failed to see in themselves. One kept faith as God kept faith with the Israelites, the stubborn stiff-necked people, complaining even at the moment of their redemption, turning their backs, endlessly squabbling, quick to forget signs and wonders. One identified with them, even at their lowest, because otherwise one would be lost. He would be lost, desolate. A man needed to belong to something greater than himself.

But the call ended with Kotler having conveyed none of this.

It was late now, approaching midnight, too late, Kotler thought, to call Benzion. Besides, he still wasn't fully accustomed to the idea that a soldier on active duty could be telephoned. On this subject, despite his having lived more than two decades in Israel, his frame of reference was seventy years out of date, rooted in childhood and his father's stories of the eastern front. These stories, supported by a few photographs and a packet of yellowed field post—folded into triangles and bearing the censor's seals—were deeply encoded in Kotler's psyche.

A movement in the window drew his eye and Kotler turned from the black absorption of the mountains. Faster than a thought, his knees buckled, responding to an overwhelming impulse to drop to the ground, to get out of sight. Kotler caught himself, and stood rigidly, his knees still slightly and comically bent. Blood battered his heart as if to dislodge it. The fear was one he'd not known in untold years. Framed in the window was a man, Svetlana's husband, arrested by some worry or introspection, his profile presented to Kotler. Kotler's thoughts swirled, sense convoluted with nonsense. He knew that the man could not see him, but he feared the man could see him. He knew the year was 2013 and that the Soviet Union no longer existed, but he felt the cold menace of the KGB, sensed the nearness of his old tormentors. He knew he was an Israeli citizen, a husband and father, a dissident champion, but he felt isolated and vulnerable, helpless to stave off the horror. In the window the man blinked his eyes and wearily ran his hand through his white hair. He cleared his throat, opened his mouth to call out to his wife, squinted as he listened for her reply, and then shuffled from the room.

FIVE

Leora was watching the television when Kotler entered the room. He caught a glimpse of the screen and recognized the movie, *White Sun of the Desert*, a Soviet film, once a personal favorite. It had come out in 1970, when he was twenty years old and taking his first tentative steps down the dissident path. He'd read a samizdat translation of Leon Uris's *Exodus*. He'd given vent in mixed company to some mildly provocative ideas. Little things. The movie's tone—dry, laconic, gently mocking of the Soviet revolutionary myths—had struck him as simpatico. And the music as well, with the famous ballad by Okudzhava, back when Kotler still considered himself a student and follower of music. Now, before Leora turned the television off, he saw the burka-clad women scurrying down the lane of the dusty Oriental town. The women in their burkas, the somnolent bearded elders, the crusading Western liberators, the primitive Muslim insurgents, the flaming oil wells; who could have predicted the immutability of this unhappy subject?

Kotler joined Leora on the bed atop the blue coverlet. The atmosphere between them at that moment was unerringly chaste. Leora held herself slightly aloof, as if in anticipation of a blow. This trip they had embarked on, already fraught with many complications, seemed to accrue new ones by the minute. Mostly, Kotler thought, because he was inept at selfishness. After a life of self-denial, he had finally pursued a selfish want, but he kept undermining himself. How long had he dreamed of sleeping with Leora in a large white room overlooking the sea? If not from the first moment he saw her, then soon after he brought her onto his staff and, increasingly, into his home. A smart and efficient girl who quickly proved her worth. She was frequently at their table for Friday-night dinners. She became like an older sister to Dafna and went shopping with her for clothes that Miriam, in her piousness, abjured. All the while, a current passed between him and Leora, like the invisible data that streamed between all the new machines. It went like this for years. Then one night a year ago, the two of them working late in his office, she had glanced up from her note-taking and caught him looking at her in an explicit way, and, for the first time, he did not draw the cloak of self-restraint. *How I have denied myself,* he said to her. *Should I continue to deny myself?* She had considered him steadily and said, *I can't answer that for you.* To which he'd replied, *Yes, you can.* And they had done in his office what so many other political men had done in theirs. For shame, Kotler thought, and yet they continued to follow in this disreputable tradition.

—What did Dafna say? Leora asked. Other than that she hates me?

—In so many words, she called her father a fool. A popular

position at the moment, and difficult to dispute. Though I disputed it.

—That's all?

—She's a grown girl. A young woman. No longer a child, as she is quick to remind me. A father doesn't fully realize this until it stares him in the face. It isn't all bad. Sooner or later, the realization arrives: the child discovers the immaturity of the parent, and the parent the maturity of his child.

—It's all wonderfully philosophical, Baruch.

—Yes, well, at times like these, we turn to our vices. The bottle for some, philosophy for others. Most of us are not blessed with your unwavering levelheadedness.

—My unwavering levelheadedness. Do you know what it's like to be a levelheaded girl? It's like having a disfigurement. I'm still embarrassed by the stupid things I did to try to overcome it.

—To me it isn't a disfigurement. Quite the contrary, I like it very much.

—That puts you in the minority. A small minority.

—Not for the first time, Kotler said and took Leora's hand.

—So that's it, then? Leora asked. Nothing has changed? We go on as before?

—Nothing has changed between us, Kotler said.

—And *not* between us? If there is something you want to say, Baruch, you should say it.

Kotler tried to draw Leora closer to him, but she held her ground, such as it was, refusing to be mollified.

—What does the name Vladimir Tankilevich mean to you? Kotler asked.

From her expression, he saw that it meant nothing. It was no surprise. The name had long ago ceased to mean anything to all but a handful of people. A dwindling handful. A few of the central players from the defining drama of Kotler's life.

—He's my red-haired Motele, Kotler said with a weary smile.

—I don't know what that means, Baruch.

—It's a line from Eugenia Ginzburg. Her first offhand impression of the man who will eventually destroy her life. "Who's the red-haired Motele?" she asks her husband at a picnic. The analogy isn't perfect. Ginzburg was a Jewish Communist and her red-haired Motele was a Jewish Chekist, but the line nevertheless stuck in my head.

—Perhaps I'm dense, Baruch, or on edge, or just tired, but I'm not in the mood for puzzles.

—Tankilevich was the man who denounced me. My old roommate in Moscow who also happened to be a KGB informant. He published the open letter in *Izvestia* that said I was working for the CIA.

—All right. What of him?

—I saw him.

—When did you see him? I've been with you all day.

—I saw him when I was standing in the yard making the phone call to Dafna. I saw him through the window of the house. Shall I go on?

There was no need for him to go on. Leora rose from the bed and looked at him soberly.

—You saw him, but did he see you?

—No.

—Fine, Leora said.

She turned from Kotler and pulled open a dresser drawer. She scooped up an armful of their clothes and dropped it in a pile at the foot of the bed. Kotler understood that she meant to rouse him to action, to counter what had already taken root in him—what she sensed had taken root in him—but it did no good. He sat serene and motionless on the bed. Leora looked at him with ebbing defiance. He could see it ebbing, flagging. Beginning at her eyes, her shoulders, her spine, and so on. Against such motionless serenity, nothing could be done. They both knew this. As for the source of the serenity that had possessed him so swiftly, Kotler was almost embarrassed to say. It was unlike the serenity with which he had confronted Amnon and the prime minister and the various foes of his past. That serenity had been the product of reason and principle, easy to articulate and, at least in his own mind, defend. This serenity descended upon him from another dimension. For want of a better word, a mystical one. Though, no doubt, this was how all irrational people justified their intransigences.

—We should never have come here, Leora said. We should never have gone with that woman. I said so.

—But we did. And, as strange as this will sound coming from my mouth, I can't help but feel that it was for a reason.

—Yes? And what reason?

—That's what I'd like to find out.

—I still don't understand. What's there to find out? You've stumbled upon the man who betrayed you forty years ago. The odds of this, of ending up a boarder in his house, are almost nil. But so? Now what? Is it that you want to exact vengeance? What is it? Do you want to hit him?

—No, those fantasies ended long ago.

—So what, then? Do you want to prove something to him? Confront him with your achievements?

—No. And it hardly feels like the moment for it.

—Doesn't it? You're on the front pages of newspapers. Yes, there's a scandal, but that's incidental. The real point is about the fate of our country, a fate that means a great deal to a great many people. And you are at the center of it. Who is he, this Tankilevich, compared to that?

—I also have a beautiful young mistress. You forgot to mention that.

—And he is married to a sly embittered hag. And he lives in this decrepit little house. And he's barely scraping by. And he's probably nursing some chronic ailment of the liver or the prostate. And, and, and…In the end, there has been some kind of justice. What more do you want?

—I'm curious, Leora. That's my only explanation. Curiosity. A curiosity deep in my bones. I'm as curious as I have ever been in my life.

—That's your entire reason?

—I want to know, Leora. First and foremost. It is a need like hunger. You satisfy the need, and the rationale, the why, comes after, once you are sated.

—And to satisfy this need you're willing to risk revealing yourself to these people? Not only that, but also us, the time we have together here. The only time like this we've ever had or may ever have. Because what do you think will happen when you confront this man and his wife? That we'll continue on as if nothing happened? That we'll go to the beach and take excursions to the Livadia Palace and the Chekhov Museum? If you confront this man, you don't know what will happen, except that we will lose our chance to be alone together as we dreamed. If that isn't important to you, if that is a subordinate need, then you will have answered a question for *me*.

The outburst brought a flush to Leora's throat and cheeks, a sensuality, as if ardor of any kind were related to sexual ardor. Kotler looked at her breathing above him and was filled with the animal instinct to pounce on her so they could claw and tear at each other. The lushness of her body still inflamed him, the fullness and smoothness of her breasts, her buttocks, her thighs. Her flesh that he stuffed his mouth with, that he clutched by the handful like a bandit. Her body, where she invited, encouraged, him to enact his every wildness, his every brackish want. Between them there was no hesitation, no apology. With Leora he had been able to be himself, the paragon of virtue, but also a man who felt the weight of his testicles under the point of his prick. A man he had only half been for forty years of prison and vindication and glory and indebtedness and fidelity and timidity. He had been locked up at twenty-five and released at thirty-eight. He had gone into prison a young man, newly wed, and he had come out a gaunt, desiccated saint. What a groom he was for the bride who had waited for him all those years. And what a bride awaited him, after her own years of dogged, confounding struggle. Two people who had long occupied cold solitary beds were brought together. Two old acquaintances, nearly strangers, were expected—by the world, by themselves— to leap into passionate embrace or slip into delicate intimacy. They had done their best. They were persistent, devoted people, and they persisted also in the matter of their hearts. In many ways, they did what everyone did to stoke the embers of the original fire. But their fire hadn't simply abated; it was practically extinguished for want of fuel, the ordinary fuel of shared days and casual contact. Apart, they had pretended that the embers still glowed, that the fire still burned, but reunited, they knew the truth. Still, they had rekindled a fire. It was no small thing. It was a real fire. But the fire you rekindle is not the same fire, doesn't burn as hot. With Leora, he burned as before, with consuming heat.

—Are you not also curious, Leora? Kotler asked. Don't you want to see what will happen? This coincidence is not mine alone. It is ours together. If we stay, what happens will include you. You will be part of it. As I believe you are meant to be. As I would like you to be. Because if greater forces have conspired, they have seen fit to include you. After all, what brought you to me started forty years ago between me and this man.

Hostage

SIX

At dawn, Chaim Tankilevich gripped the metal handrail and pulled himself into the trolleybus, which, with its wobbly antennae, resembled an old, dun grasshopper. He handed the driver his fare, fifteen hryvnia, and lumbered to take one of the vacant seats in the rear of the vehicle. This was not hard to do. All of the seats were vacant and would remain so for much of the trip. He was going against the current. At the other end, in Simferopol, a crowd was boarding a trolleybus to come to the sea, but in Yalta he was among a dismal handful who, for their own insular reasons, were going in the wrong direction. And of these, only he appeared every Saturday, summer or winter, rain or shine, year after year, now for ten years. Occasionally, over this time, some misfortune had led one or another person to undertake this journey for a period of weeks or months—a man who required a course of chemotherapy at a specialized clinic; a woman who succored her ailing mother and then her ailing aunt. Their appearance on the trolleybus was temporal, tragically temporal, as his appearance was tragically permanent.

But this wasn't something he disclosed to his co-sufferers. He presented them instead with a similar tale of woe. He was going to visit his brother, once a successful businessman, now destitute and homebound, crippled by gangsters. This was something that ordinary people could understand. To tell them the truth, that he was going to Simferopol because it was Shabbat, because there weren't enough Jewish men in Simferopol willing or able to come to synagogue—this seemed a bizarre and inadvisable thing to disclose. He had no desire to engage in ethnography or explain himself. Besides, to fully explain himself would have been impossible. Better and easier to tell a total than a partial falsehood.

The trip to Simferopol took three hours—trundling across the flats, creeping up the rises, passed by every other vehicle. It was particularly so in these, the oldest of the trolleybuses, relics still from the Khrushchev era. But it was true even in the newer ones—every model a different color, lest someone confuse decades and regimes—all of them lugubrious grasshoppers. Back and forth they went along this triumph of Soviet engineering, the longest trolleybus line in the world. A typical Soviet triumph: scale over substance.

So many times had Tankilevich made this trip that he believed he had memorized every square meter of the terrain. Now it was summer. He could anticipate every roadside stand with its jars of honey and strings of purple Yalta onions. He could anticipate the sloping vineyards and the pastures with their cows and horses like indolent fixtures of the landscape. And he could anticipate the cement bus shelters and the blank-eyed men who sat on their haunches beside them. This pitiless monotony, this drone of a life, to this he had been condemned. Especially in this land, to this they had all been condemned. The fortunate among them were able to shirk the knowledge, to keep it in abeyance. But this was denied him. Deliberately and vengefully denied him. He was forced to look, to contend with the unremitting dreariness of existence. He was a seventy-year-old man afflicted with cataracts, arrhythmia, and sciatica, captive of the trolleybus, tormented body and soul.

Tankilevich didn't think he could go on this way much longer. He had told Svetlana that he was at the end of his rope.

—And after you dangle from your rope, what then? Then it's my turn?

—I can't do it anymore, Tankilevich said. Simply, I am going crazy.

—Then go before Nina Semonovna and fall on your knees.

And that was what he intended to do. He had telephoned Nina Semonovna and requested an audience. A busy, taciturn woman, she had of course asked if they couldn't transact their business over the telephone, but Tankilevich had held firm. The matter was too delicate, too weighty for the telephone. It could be done only in person. Grudgingly, she agreed—as though she surmised what he wanted but consented, against her better judgment, to see him anyway.

From the trolleybus terminal Tankilevich caught a small local bus that brought him within a kilometer of the synagogue. Fifteen hryvnia for the trolleybus and three hryvnia for the local bus, a total of thirty-six hryvnia for the round-trip. Four times a month, it totaled nearly a hundred and fifty hryvnia, equivalent to twenty American dollars. The entire monthly subsidy he and Svetlana received from the Hesed was one hundred dollars. So one-fifth of their subsidy was squandered just to transport his carcass to and from the synagogue. The pain of this also never abated.

It was now just past nine in the morning. Services were technically scheduled to begin around this time. When Tankilevich had first started coming to synagogue, they had still sometimes managed to draw the quorum required by Jewish law. But even then they had engaged in a pantomime. By rights, with ten men, they were entitled to read from the Torah, but they never did. They had a Torah—the scrolls donated by Jews in Evanston, Illinois—but none of them had the training to read from it. Out of a sense of piety and obligation, they would unlatch the ark to reveal the scrolls. Once a year, on Simchas Torah, they would remove them from the ark. They would open a bottle of vodka, shoulder the scrolls, and dance with them to the accompaniment of whatever Hebrew and Yiddish songs they could improvise. But Tankilevich couldn't remember when they'd last assembled ten men. If they unlatched the ark now, it was from a habit transmuted into tradition. They didn't know if it was strictly permissible to look upon the scrolls in the absence of a quorum, let alone to touch them. But they were operating under hard constraints and believed that the Almighty would tolerate and forgive.

To walk the kilometer was never pleasant. In summer, even at nine in the morning, the heat could already be burdensome. By the time Tankilevich arrived at the synagogue, his handkerchief would be wet. In the winter, if it snowed, the way was slick and treacherous. In the spring and fall, there were cold, spiteful rains. But in any season, even in the mildest weather, there was still nothing to enjoy about the trek. The neighborhood where the synagogue stood was one of the worst in Simferopol. Even by the deplorable standards of the time, the roads and sidewalks were in terrible disrepair. So too the houses—huddled, dark, flaking and eroding. Trees and weeds grew wild. Refuse littered the streets. Cadaverous old women and dogs picked through it. Beginning in the afternoon, local toughs emerged, drinking and cursing. Into this midst many Jews were reluctant to come. Of those who did, their numbers were shrinking. It was a matter of attrition. When one of them departed—now almost exclusively in the eternal sense—nobody replaced him. They had counted seven men. Then six. And now, with the death of Isidor Feldman, five. Not including Manya Grinblatt and Shura Feyn, the two women.

Past a parked van and a broken chair, Tankilevich reached the synagogue. Its exterior was crumbling, the paint on its wooden window frames blistered. To gain entry, one went around to the side and through an iron gate wide enough to admit a car. On Saturday mornings, this was left unlocked. Then the narrow lane that separated the synagogue from the neighboring house—an ordinary residence like all the other residences on the street. The synagogue was tucked away, secreted here as in meaner times. Unless someone knew different, there was nothing to identify the house. Only the Jewish faces that doddered in on Saturday mornings.

Like the gate, the side door was also unlocked. Beyond, there was a dim cool hallway that offered Tankilevich his first instance of relief. The house may have been in a sorry state, but it had been properly built, close to a century ago, with walls thick enough to contend with the extremes of the climate. A few steps and he could hear more clearly the voices in the prayer room. Voices raised not in prayer but in routine, familiar disputation.

Tankilevich pulled open the door and saw them. He thought, *Here they are, my companions of ten years. God grant I not see them again until I choose.*

He went to his customary place, at the rearmost of two dark mahogany tables. Each table had three chairs. Normally Isidor Feldman and Hilka Berezov, Nina Semonovna's brother, occupied the two other seats at his table. But Isidor had died of a stroke that past Tuesday, and Hilka, at fifty-four the youngest and most affluent among them, had closed the electronics shop he owned near the train station and taken his wife and children for a week to Kerch. So Tankilevich had the table to himself. Moshe Podolsky, the elderly Nahum Ziskin, and Nahum's son Pinya were at the other table, nearest to the bimah, from which the Torah was intended to be read. To their right, on chairs positioned against the wall, in an approximation of a separate section, were Manya Grinblatt and Shura Feyn.

Golden light poured into the room through four tall arched windows on the opposite wall. In this light—and in the light of his imminent leave-taking—the prayer room and its occupants were nobly cast. The shabbiness that marked the rest of the building and the neighborhood was not to be found here. The mahogany tables and chairs were sturdy, built for epochs. The bimah and the ark beyond it had already withstood the darkest times. Somehow they had been rescued from the conflagration. The bimah—a raised platform and table— was lacquered black wood with flashes of gold. The ark was the same, gilded and carved, its doors concealed behind a burgundy velvet curtain trimmed, tasseled, and embroidered in gold. Above hung two crystal chandeliers. The walls were whitewashed, the room clean. And of his companions, awash in this light? History had laid its heavy hand on them, but they had burrowed, eluded, resisted, and remained. One needed only to look at their faces—expressive Jewish faces—to see that they had known the depths of life. Let no one say that he lacked feelings for these people and this place, Tankilevich thought. Neither was he deserting them. Deserting them for what? He would be the one with the void in his life.

Moshe Podolsky was jabbing the air with his finger as Tankilevich lowered himself into his seat.

—This, this is precisely why I left that country! Podolsky declared.

Tankilevich immediately grasped the substance of the conversation. Israel. His blood quickened.

Podolsky, in his olive army cap, had risen from his chair to more emphatically make his point to the two Ziskins and the women who followed the discussion from their places along the wall. A minute turn of his head, and Podolsky now included Tankilevich as well.

—What do the Arabs do? They throw rocks. They attack innocent women and children. They shoot rockets. If they pay a few shekels in tax, where does the money go? To their crooked Palestinian officials, who, if such a thing is possible, are more corrupt than our Ukrainian ones. Meanwhile, the Jews pay money to the state. In Israel, they pay taxes, and from America they send how many millions. And what does the state do with this money? It commands Jewish soldiers to evict Jews from their homes.

—Of course, Nahum Ziskin said, it's only in Israel if a Jew builds a house it's a crime.

Even more than the prayers, Tankilevich would miss such

conversations. With whom else could he speak this way? In Yalta, surrounded by goyim, he could talk like this only to himself. To speak like this even with Svetlana was to stir up turbulent feelings.

Podolsky, born Mihail but reconsecrated as Moshe, had lived in Israel for three years in the late 1990s before returning to Simferopol. His reasons for returning, Tankilevich still found murky. Podolsky ascribed his departure to his frustration with the state, its pandering to the Americans and the Arabs at the expense of the Jews. Was this reason enough for a person to leave a country like Israel and return to one like Ukraine? But Tankilevich, given his own biographical infelicities, did not pry. In this country, at this point in time, a man was entitled to his secrets, his fabrications. If Podolsky gave as his reason for leaving the ideological incongruities between himself and the state of Israel, then it was best not to scrutinize too closely. If it seemed odd that Podolsky, still ardent in his Zionism, when restrained from living in Judaea or Samaria, had opted for Simferopol over Jerusalem or Haifa, it was best to regard this as no more than a personal quirk. The man had been in his middle forties when he'd returned. He had a wife and son. The economic situation in Crimea in the 1990s had been even worse than it was now. Would a man hazard such a move based purely on political discontent? Since then, Podolsky's son had, of his own accord, re-immigrated to Israel. But Podolsky had stayed. Tankilevich knew it wasn't because he was prospering. He was a heating technician; his wife was a bank teller. What held them? It wasn't love for Crimea, Ukraine, Russians, or Tatars. Podolsky's life revolved around Judaism and Israel. He oversaw the synagogue, unlocking the doors every Saturday morning. He wore his olive army cap in solidarity with the Jewish settlers. He kept abreast of the latest developments in Israel, even reading the Hebrew newspapers on his computer. Tankilevich was not alone in wondering what precisely had happened to Podolsky in Israel. What act had he committed that kept him from returning to the place where his heart so clearly resided?

The question of Israel, of why they had not relocated there, pertained to them all. Why did they persist here? Nahum Ziskin was eighty-five years old. Too old to leave, too old to make a new start. Pinya, his son, had never married and, with a mental deficiency, had never lived apart. What would become of him when Nahum died? They were sustained now mostly by Nahum's German reparations. When Nahum was gone, that money would cease. Manya Grinblatt's husband was Ukrainian and had no desire to live in Israel. Shura Feyn, a widow, was as old as Nahum Ziskin and frail. Her daughter had married a Russian and moved to Siberia. Hilka Berezov had been deliberating for years whether to stay or go, his inclinations fluctuating with the fortunes of his electronics business. And Isidor Feldman, a man with a sense of humor, always maintained that he would have left long ago if he hadn't already bought a plot next to his wife at the Jewish cemetery and didn't want some stranger taking his place. Now this was no longer an issue.

—The Israeli government is nothing but a Judenrat! Podolsky declaimed. If anyone doubted it before, it should be clear now. The Americans and the Arabs issue the order, and their Jewish servants carry it out. They deceive themselves with the same rotten Judenrat logic. "If only we do this, our masters will be satisfied. If only we sacrifice these few, they will spare the rest." Have not enough books been written on this subject? Is this some obscure wrinkle of history? What is the point of this Yad Vashem? So the Polish pope and the Nazi pope can have a nice place to go make a speech? And when the Arabs take over? When the Judenrat gives them Jerusalem? Then what will happen to this Yad Vashem?

—It will become the Zionist Occupation Museum, Tankilevich said, braced with tribal feeling.

—If not a mosque, said Nahum Ziskin.

This was what it was like to be on firm spiritual footing. To enjoy the prerogative of every human being: the society of like-minded fellows. In whose midst a man understood things preternaturally, in his bones. Yes, as if, after a fashion, the neural threads led to a common brain, the vessels to a common heart. Where even disagreement was disagreement within yourself. Once connected, always connected. Nothing and no one, exerting even the greatest power, could refute this.

For another fifteen minutes they remonstrated about this newest Israeli crisis, as though it were part of the liturgy they had come to recite. Then again, what were their prayers for? What was the point of Jewish prayer? What was the point of it from the very beginning? One point: Zion. A return to Zion. The ingathering of the scattered people at Zion. The arrival of the messianic age and the rebuilding of the temple in Zion. When there were millions under the tsar, it was for Zion. Now that there was but this puny remnant, it could only be for Zion. Even in London, New York, and Dnepropetrovsk, where they were not living under the shadow of extinction, it was still for Zion. Only in Zion was it not for Zion.

SEVEN

After services, Tankilevich didn't linger as he often did but hurried out on the pretext of seeing his daughter. Often on these Saturdays, he visited her and her husband in the apartment they rented in a different, marginally less squalid, part of the city. For these visits Svetlana outfitted him with a parcel of food—even if only a jar of preserves and a few eggs from their chicken coop. Depending on how things sat, Tankilevich might also slip in fifty hryvnia. In return, his daughter did him the service of going once a month to pick up his Hesed subsidy. But today, because of his fearsome meeting with Nina Semonovna, he had avoided making other plans. He reasoned that if the meeting went well, he could still call his daughter and arrange to see her. But if the meeting went badly, he was certain that he would be in no condition to see her or anyone else. He dreaded to think about the condition he would be in if the meeting went badly.

Nina Semonovna had set their meeting at her office at the Hesed. She did not normally come in on Saturdays, the Hesed being closed on Shabbat, but she was making this accommodation for him. Tankilevich knew he was inconveniencing her and that this would not incline her favorably toward him, but what other choice did he have? Ten years earlier, when he had first contacted her, he had insisted on meeting after business hours, when he could be assured that nobody would overhear them. He supposed he could have done the same again, but it seemed to him that making his petition at the end of a long workday was no better than making it in the middle of a quiet Saturday. Besides, on another day he would have had to make an additional trip to Simferopol, six more hours on the hard plastic seats of the trolleybus; the prospect was too dispiriting, too daunting.

It was nearly forty-five minutes from the synagogue to the Hesed. There was the walk to the bus stop, a series of two minibuses to wait for, and another ten-minute walk to the apartment building where, on the ground floor, the Hesed had its offices. A wealthy American Jew with roots in Simferopol had bought the building and lent them the space. They were lucky to have it. Other communities—the Tatars, the Ukrainians—had nothing at all, even though there were plenty of rich Arabs in the Gulf and rich Ukrainians in Canada. Still, the location was problematic. Aside from the synagogue that Tankilevich attended, there were two others in the city, a Reformist and a Chabad—both struggling, both far from the Hesed. Nina Semonovna's big ambition, known to all, was to reclaim the old Talmud Torah building, erected in 1913 to educate Jewish boys. It was large and well situated, perfect for a center. With such a building, the community might stand a chance. But for many years, it had served as the Institute of Sport. In the 1990s, the government had returned some buildings to local communities, but there was little chance it would return this one. The state was poor and the Jews were poor. What did moral and historical claims matter in such an equation? So the Gestapo had used it as their headquarters. So they had collected Jews there before sending them to their macabre deaths. But the innocent students of the Institute of Sport hadn't done this. Why should they be dispossessed?

A crime demanded rectification! That was why. But it would never happen.

The situation was not bound to improve. They had just said the kaddish for Isidor Feldman. A sad business in and of itself, made sadder by the fact that without Feldman they were further depleted. Their trajectory was ineluctable. During the prayer, the perverse thought had occurred to Tankilevich that they could have used Feldman's voice to help say the kaddish for Feldman.

Tankilevich rang the bell to be admitted into the Hesed and waited for some time for a response. He rang again and then felt, through the door, the reverberations of someone's steps striding toward him. A turn of the bolt and Nina Semonovna was there. A handsome Jewish woman in her fifties, of the Portuguese type, olive-skinned, full-featured, and without a shred of credulity, habituated to a deceitful, grasping world where everyone is suspect. Tankilevich was no exception.

Dispensing with *Hello* she said, Come in.

He followed her through the empty reception area where the guard usually sat. Then through the narrow corridor, dim because she had not bothered to turn on the lights. Along the walls were posted the displays. There was always something. Tankile-

vich remembered one that featured Jewish Nobel laureates—
Einstein, Bohr, Pasternak, and so on—complete with their like-
nesses and short biographies. Now it was local Jewish war heroes:
soldiers, sailors, and partisans. Affixed to the walls were dozens of
photographs; some depicted the fighters in their youth, some in
their later years. They passed the doors to the lecture room, the
doors to the library, the doors to the game room. At the end of
the corridor, Nina Semonovna indicated a padded vinyl chair situated in front of the door to the administrative offices.

—Wait here, please, she said morosely, I have another client.

Tankilevich did as he was told. He sat in the dim corridor
and, almost in spite of himself, caught strains of the dispute
that resounded behind the closed door: Nina Semonovna's firm,
even tone and another, shriller female voice. Nina Semonovna's
words were difficult to distinguish but, Tankilevich could make
out some of the other woman's phrases at the highest pitch:
*On whose authority? …How dare you? …Who said so? …I am
entitled!*

After this appetizer, Tankilevich thought, what stomach for
the main course?

There followed a considerable period of silence broken by
one final proclamation and the harsh scraping of chair legs.
Then the door flew open and a woman barged furiously out. She
was about the same age as Nina Semonovna, stout and heavy-
bosomed. She passed him with hardly a glance, only a flash of
gold earrings and a swirl of her long skirt. She stamped her
heels on the linoleum and Tankilevich felt shudders through
the base of his chair. There was also the echo, like cannonade.
Meanwhile, Nina Semonovna filled the doorway and observed
laconically the woman's departure.

—If you would be so kind as to close the door behind you, she called after her.

She waited calmly for the sound of the slamming door and then turned her attention to Tankilevich.

—Now, Nina Semonovna said, what can I do for you?

Tankilevich followed her into the office and took the seat she indicated. He watched her round her desk.

—If once, only once, someone would ask for a meeting to express their gratitude, Nina Semonovna said as she sat down across from Tankilevich. Yes? If someone was so overcome with gratitude for what we do here that he simply had to come in and say so. That would be something.

Tankilevich could think of no satisfactory response. Nor did he believe that one was expected of him.

Nina Semonovna gazed at him with bemusement.

—Of course, if one wishes to hear *Thank you,* one should seek another line of work.

Once more, Tankilevich could think of no response short of nodding his head.

—You don't happen to know that woman? Nina Semonovna asked.

—I don't, Tankilevich replied honestly. He was certain he'd never seen her before.

—She owns two shops, she and her husband. Also a small apartment building. Everyone knows this. But she comes here outraged that I have denied her claim for support. What is my explanation? My explanation, naturally, is that I am not going to be taken for a fool. She insists she is destitute. She owns nothing. Preposterous to accuse her of owning shops and a building. Her daughter owns these. All the documents are in the daughter's name. In case I doubt it, she waves the documents. So on what *grounds* and by what *authority* am I denying her claim? On what grounds and by what authority? On the grounds of conscience and by the authority of common decency. And you saw the result.

Nina Semonovna felt around the tabletop for her pack of cigarettes. Nimbly, she pulled one from the pack and lit it. She held the cigarette in her hand and allowed a tendril of smoke to curl past her eyes.

—Now I can look forward to a complaint from this person to the Odessa Hesed. And, I assure you, I *do* look forward to it. The shame of it is that for a person like her, there are no consequences. She will make her outrageous demands, and I—and other people who have far more important things to do—will have no choice but to suffer them. And in the end she will get what she wants. Because even though everyone knows she's a liar, on paper she has covered her fat arse. It's because of behavior like this that people detest Jews. Because of this miserable shrewdness and greed. I won't say it doesn't exist. In my position, I see my share. But for every one like her, there are twenty others who honestly don't have two kopeks to rub together. And when this woman takes money to which she has absolutely no right, when she cheats and steals, it's not from me that she steals, but from them. So even if there's nothing I can do to stop her, I can at least take some pleasure in blackening her days. I don't fool myself into thinking that this will cause her to reconsider or repent—with such people, one learns not to expect moral transformations—but it will send the message that when you come into this office with the intention to deceive, you will not be able to simply waltz in and out, but you will take it on the head!

Nina Semonovna put her cigarette to her lips and inhaled. If the point of her monologue had been to discourage him, Tankilevich thought, she had succeeded. Nevertheless, he didn't have a choice. He'd come with a realistic appraisal of his prospects. Nina Semonovna had done nothing but confirm what he had already suspected. But so? His part was to ask. And her part, then, was to deny. If nothing else, at least he, unlike the woman, was not engaged in fraud. He wasn't concealing anything. Between him and Nina Semonovna, everything was out in the open. At once out in the open and closely guarded. That was what he believed—though this display of hers, the zeal with which she revealed to him the details of another client's case, raised apprehensions. Here he was, proposing to go back on his word, but could it be that she had long since gone back on hers? Then again, in all these years he had seen nothing to suggest that she had misled him. He would have sensed it if people knew the truth about his past. It was not the kind of information someone could possess and dismiss. Certainly not Jews. Certainly not Jews like her brother and the others at the synagogue. Which led him to believe that Nina Semonovna had, at least in his case, remained discreet.

As Tankilevich girded himself to speak, Nina Semonovna took another pull on her cigarette and said, But you didn't come to hear me complain.

—I appreciate your difficulties, Tankilevich said, and do not wish to add to them. But I have come to talk about the synagogue.

—Yes, the synagogue, Nina Semonovna said grimly.

—You probably know that Isidor Feldman died.

—A good person, Nina Semonovna said. One of the last with

roots in the farming colonies. I meant to go to the funeral, but it was one thing after another.

—Yes, a good person, Tankilevich said. A loss to the community, and also to the synagogue. He came regularly. Without him there are only five men left.

—This is our predicament. Our people go and we can't replace them. But I don't suppose you have come here with a solution?

—I regret—I regret sincerely—that I have not, Tankilevich said and felt the heat of desperation rise on his skin. He imagined Nina Semonovna could detect it from where she sat.

—If you regret, then you are sitting in the right place. The place of regret. This is where everyone comes with their regrets. Regrets, of course, that are really requests. Or am I mistaken?

Tankilevich held a chastened silence.

—So let's get to it, then, Nina Semonovna said. What do you want?

—It isn't a matter of what I want, Tankilevich said. What I want and what, unfortunately, I am able to do are two different things.

Nina Semonovna crossed her hands on the desktop and gazed bitterly at Tankilevich.

—It is a Saturday, Mr. Tankilevich. I have just been yelled at by a hideous woman. My patience for games and intrigues is thin.

—Ten years ago, I came to see you for the first time. I wonder if you remember.

—I remember very well. Even with my long and varied experience, it is hard to forget a case like yours.

—So you remember our agreement?

—To the letter.

—I have honored this agreement for ten years. I have not missed so much as a single Saturday.

—Very good. Are you here for my congratulations?

—Nina Semonovna, I think you will agree that ten years is a long time. I was sixty then; I am seventy now.

—And I trust you will soon get to the point.

—Ten years ago, when we made our agreement, there were still enough men for the minyan. But for a long time that hasn't been so. With me or without me, the number will not reach ten.

The ash had grown at the tip of Nina Semonovna's cigarette. Without taking her eyes from Tankilevich, she tapped it into a crude ceramic ashtray, a children's craft project with a purple Star of David painted at its center. Then, implacably and unhurriedly, she brought the remainder of the cigarette to her lips. She released the smoke and continued to regard Tankilevich as if from a predatory height.

—Despite what you might think, Nina Semonovna, it was not easy for me to come here. I have endured for a long time the hardship that our agreement has imposed on me. I have endured it and accepted it as my obligation and my lot. But I am an old man now. My health is not what it once was. My vision is bad. My heart troubles me. I have sciatica that makes sitting for hours on the trolleybus a kind of torture. These trips to and from Yalta are taking their toll on me, Nina Semonovna. A toll both physical and psychological. A toll that, I believe, no longer has a justification.

Nina Semonovna ground her cigarette into the ashtray.

—So we have finally reached the point? You would like to be

released from your obligations? On account of the terrible hardships imposed, yes?

—I would.

—And what about my part of our agreement? Am I then to be released from that?

Tankilevich eyed Nina Semonovna cautiously.

—You speak of the hardship our agreement imposed on you, but why not ask about the hardship it imposed on me? Do you think it was easy for me to engage in this subterfuge all these years? And to engage in it for the sake of a person like you?

Nina Semonovna leaned forward, her eyes lit with malice. But also with something else. A kind of gladness. He had been mistaken. The appetizer hadn't robbed her of a stomach for the main course. Quite the contrary. It had whetted her appetite. The appetizer had made her ravenous, eager to devour something. It was likely that, even without the episode with the horrible woman, Nina Semonovna would have denied his request. But after the horrible woman, his fate was sealed. Such was his misfortune.

—You ask if I remember when you first came to this office. When I say I remember, not only do I mean that I remember it now because you have asked me to. When I say I remember, I mean that I have never forgotten. I mean that, from time to time, I still think about you, Mr. Tankilevich. I still think about you and whether I was right or wrong to enter into this arrangement with you. Because I did not like you from the first. I did not like you and I did not trust you. I thought you were an opportunist. That is still my opinion. Because of what you did for the KGB, because of how you conducted yourself in the decades after, because of the circumstances under which you came to my office, I thought you deserved nothing but scorn. Not my indulgence, not my protection, and not a kopek of the Hesed's money.

—I see, Nina Semonovna, Tankilevich said. And ten years of my faithful attendance at the synagogue has not changed your opinion?

—Why should it? You attended only for the Hesed subsidy. What is there to admire, Mr. Tankilevich? It is *batlanus,* and you are a *batlan.* I am not happy that I had to resort to *batlanus* to help the synagogue, but that is our reality. Hilka complained to me that they did not have enough men and by chance you happened on my doorstep. So I extended my offer. More out of sentiment than sense. Always a mistake. As you have now proved.

—I'm sorry, but how exactly have I proved this? By making a difficult trip from Yalta to Simferopol for ten years, until my health no longer permits it? You think I did all that as part of some fraud? The fraud, Nina Semonovna, was my life until I came to you.

Nina Semonovna leaned back and emitted a throaty, contemptuous laugh. She laughed this way, deliberately, overlong, until the laugh drained to a dark smile.

—Quite a declaration, Mr. Tankilevich. You'll forgive me if I don't applaud. But since you put it like this, allow me to say you could have put an end to the so-called fraud of your life at any time simply by walking through this door and declaring: *My name is Vladimir Tankilevich. I have reached my pensionable age. I am a Jew, descended from Jews. I was born on such and such a date, in such and such a place. Here are my sup-*

porting documents. This is what everybody else does. But this was *not* what you did. You came here under a shroud of secrecy and asked me to help you conceal your true identity. And in the moment I agreed to that, I became a party to this deception. I compromised myself for you. I could say *for the synagogue,* but this fine distinction would not count for much in the heat of a scandal. You have thought only about yourself and your situation, but allow me to enlighten you about mine. From the performance you witnessed a few minutes ago, you might have gathered that I am a person who is not without enemies. Can you imagine what that wonderful woman would do if she learned that for ten years I have been secretly helping a person like you? A notorious traitor to the Jewish people? You think she would keep quiet? You think she wouldn't be writing to Odessa and Moscow and New York to denounce me? Here I am, denying her humble claim, while I am giving money to Vladimir Tankilevich, KGB informant, the man responsible for sending the great Baruch Kotler to the Gulag. How do you think this would be received by my superiors? And by *their* superiors? By the American Jews in New York whose job it is to raise the money for our sustenance? Do you know how they do this? By appealing to their wealthy brethren who still harbor quiverings for their shtetl roots. By telling them sad tales about our existence. By printing brochures with photographs and touching descriptions of poor, neglected Russian Jews. By staging lavish events for millionaires where famous Jews, like your Baruch Kotler, make speeches to get them to open their wallets. Now, can you imagine what happens if it is revealed that some Nina Semonovna Shreibman, director of the Simferopol Hesed, has, with full and deliberate knowledge, been aiding and abetting the traitor Tankilevich, this disgrace to the Jewish people? That for ten years she has been giving him money—and not only him but also his shiksa wife? That to this end, she has manipulated documents? Are you getting the picture, Mr. Tankilevich? Can you imagine what would happen if this information was to be publicized? Not only what would happen to me. That should be quite clear. But the harm it could do to the larger structure upon which we all rely? Can you imagine how such an embarrassment would look printed in the newspapers? You have no idea how sensitive these American Jewish organizations are. Or how territorial. I have seen them go into fits over far lesser things. There are many organizations and they are all competing for the same dollars. If one group stumbles, believe me, the others are quick to take advantage. And just like that, money that has been painstakingly solicited for the Jews of Ukraine is now diverted to some other, less controversial, cause, like teaching Ethiopian Jews to eat with forks or sending young American Jews to pick tomatoes in the Negev. And all this because I stuck my neck out for you. So while you have been riding the trolleybus, Mr. Tankilevich, this is what has been hanging over my head.

Tankilevich received the speech as if it were a clobbering, and he slumped down accordingly. And yet, he thought: *Clobbered, yes, but not beaten!* In his life he had known real terrors, real bloodlettings. So this was nothing new. Unpleasant, yes, but it would take more to make him fold. He found his voice.

—Nina Semonovna, I don't dispute anything you say. But the fact remains: What choice did I have? As Vladimir Tarasov—

with this false identity bestowed upon me by the KGB—I could rejoin the community of my people. As this aberration, Vladimir Tarasov, I could attend the synagogue. And as Vladimir *Tankilevich,* I could not.

—As Vladimir Tarasov, this aberration—as you call it—you could have rejoined your community and attended the synagogue a long time ago. Nothing was stopping you. But you came only when there was money for the taking. And now you wish to have everything: to retain the disguise of Vladimir Tarasov, keep the subsidy, and retreat from your obligations to the community and the synagogue. But, Mr. Tankilevich, hear me well: So long as I sit behind this desk, I will not allow this to happen. If you do not fulfill the terms of our agreement, I will cut you off. Doing so, as you should by now understand, would be a great relief for me. A great relief and no small satisfaction.

With this statement of finality, Nina Semonovna reached again for her pack of cigarettes and, in a flare of punctuation, struck a match.

Tankilevich regarded her across the desk. She looked contented, the cigarette smoking between her fingers.

He remembered Svetlana's words. Now, then, he thought. So the time had come to go to the farthest extreme.

Stiffly—not without difficulty—he rose from his chair and pushed it from him. Its legs scraped, and the sound shot like a current along his calves and up his back. Gripping the edge of the desk, he lowered himself until the points of his knees met the hard ground. When he felt steady enough, he removed his hands from the desk and let them dangle at his sides. He lifted his eyes to Nina Semonovna, his inquisitor. This was the posture, but it was not enough. More was required. There were also the words.

—I beg of you, Tankilevich said.

Nina Semonovna gazed down at him from her bastion.

—Stand up, Mr. Tankilevich. If you are fit enough to do this, you are fit enough to go to the synagogue.

EIGHT

On Mayakovsky Street, in the center of the city, was a Furshet grocery market where, each week, Tankilevich bought provisions to take back to Yalta. The Hesed had an arrangement with the market's owners. It had a similar arrangement with a Furshet in Yalta, but Nina Semonovna deliberately hadn't put him on its roll. To utilize the subsidy, Tankilevich was obliged to do it in Simferopol. For this reason, the shopping also fell to him on these Saturdays. But after his encounter with Nina Semonovna, he felt leaden, nearly killed. How could he force himself to go to the market, to put one plodding foot in front of the other, to contemplate the bins and the shelves and be surrounded by the gaudy, mindless, mocking display of excess? His hands felt as if they were filled with sand. It would take a superhuman effort to lift them, to coax his fingers to grasp the cartons and boxes. His every fiber revolted against this. It was too much to ask of him on such a day. He pictured Svetlana's dour, disapproving expression. But what right could she invoke? She was not shackled to the trolleybus; she had not thrown herself before Nina Semonovna. The depredations were all on his head. Svetlana could stuff her disapproval. He would not go, that's all, Tankilevich thought. He would not go! But by then he was already there.

Mechanically, Tankilevich moved through the aisles, depositing their staples into a red plastic basket: bread, farmer's cheese, sour cream, cereals, buckwheat kasha, carrot juice, smoked mackerel, tomatoes, cucumbers, potatoes, green onions. A few yellow plums, because they were in season and inexpensive. He finished at the meat counter, where the woman reflexively asked, Three hundred grams roast turkey? Tankilevich had long assumed that they stocked the turkey solely for the Jews. Everything else at the counter, the appetizing salamis and sausages, contained pork and was thus forbidden under the Hesed subsidy. For pork and shellfish, as for cigarettes and alcohol, one had to lay out one's own money.

From the meat counter Tankilevich carried his basket—the plastic handle biting into his fingers, the sinews straining in his shoulder—to the cash register at the front of the market. Since it was a Saturday afternoon, the market was not short of customers. Three women stood in line ahead of him. And immediately after Tankilevich assumed his place, people formed up behind. He glanced back to take their measure. Directly behind him was a young mother with a small daughter, three or four years old, in a bright cotton dress with a white cotton cap. Behind them was an older man, Tankilevich's age, with short bristly white hair, ethnically Russian. And behind him was another man, younger than the Russian, swarthy, Tatar or Azeri, a laborer, wearing a sleeveless shirt, the taut muscles of his arms exposed. Paying for his purchases, this final element of the task, always put Tankilevich's nerves on edge, made him exceedingly conscious of the people around him, of attracting their attention, judgment, and disdain. It was the moment when he was forced to shed the bleary status of ordinary citizen and declare himself conspicuously, in blazing letters, a Jew.

Tankilevich's turn came. He presented the contents of his basket to the cashier, a blond woman in her thirties. Like the woman at the meat counter, she was offhandedly familiar with him. With quick, practiced movements she unloaded his basket and punched the prices into her register. When the sum appeared on the computerized display, the woman looked at Tankilevich and said, Coupons? It was at this point that Tankilevich became supremely attuned to any change in the atmosphere, like a dog sniffing for storm ions. And as he withdrew the bright, multicolored Hesed bills from his pocket, he picked up rumblings behind him. The air grew dense. Its sullen weight pressed on his shoulders. He turned around to confirm his suspicions. The woman behind him was gazing off, her little girl waiting docilely at her hip. Neither of them was the source of the disturbance and neither seemed to have noticed anything awry. Why should they? Tankilevich thought. Such storms did not affect them. But after a lifetime of such storms, he rarely mistook them. One look at the Russian man's face and Tankilevich knew that he wasn't mistaken now either. He saw the sneer—the bitter, arrogant, Jew-hating sneer. Locking eyes with Tankilevich, the man allowed his sneer to ripen into a smirk.

—Is there a problem? Tankilevich asked him.

The question seemed to fill the man with glee, as if Tankilevich had uttered a tremendous joke. The man swiveled his head from side to side, seeking to include others in this hilarity. If not his goggling about, then Tankilevich's question had already drawn people's attention. The young mother pulled her daughter closer and eyed both Tankilevich and the Russian warily. The cashier shifted a hip, tilted her head. And the laborer looked up with the coolness of a lizard.

—*Is there a problem?* the Russian mimicked. Not for the likes of you. Never.

—What are you implying, Citizen?

—Implying? I'm not implying anything. I'm stating what is clear as day. You people always know how to get ahead.

—You people. What people do you mean? Tankilevich demanded. If you're going to sow slander, at least have the courage to speak plainly.

—To say what I'm saying requires no courage, the Russian said. Only eyes in your head. Anyone with eyes in his head sees how you Jews always get special treatment. Isn't that so?

The Russian turned for confirmation to the people around him. But they remained silent. Tankilevich thought he even detected a hint of disapproval on the cashier's face. Still, he expected no support. How many times had he encountered such anti-Semites, and how many times had anyone said even a single word in his defense? He felt his heart pounding as if to fly apart. He gripped tightly the bills in his hand and held them up.

—What special treatment? Tankilevich said. Do you mean these?

The Russian was unintimidated.

—Who but Jews have such things? I too would like such privileges. But it's only the Jews that get them.

—You would like such privileges? Tankilevich boomed. Then

you should have lined up in '41, when the Germans were taking the Jews to the forest!

—Oh ho! the Russian said. So it's back to the Germans, is it? To listen to you people, you'd think it was only the Jews who suffered. Everyone suffered. Who shed more blood than the Russian people? But nobody gives us special favors, do they?

At this, he turned again to the others for reinforcement. First to the young mother, whose expression remained wary and reticent. And then to the laborer.

—Isn't that so, pal? the Russian asked.

The laborer took his time and then answered in Tatar-accented Russian, the consonants rolling like stones in his mouth.

—Yes, everyone suffered, he said. But not only from the Germans.

—Oh, I see, the Russian announced grandly. I'm surrounded by persecuted minorities. That's the way it is now in this country. The Russian nation built up this land—what didn't we do?—but now we're everyone's bastard. We're supposed to go around with our heads bowed and beg forgiveness from this one and the other.

The Russian had worked himself up now and gazed about defiantly, no longer expecting solidarity. He glared at Tankilevich.

—The hell I'll beg forgiveness from the likes of you! While you get special money and I have a hole in my pocket. The Germans could have lined up a few more of you in '41!

There it was, Tankilevich thought. The fuse had been lit and now the charge had detonated. His heart surged. He waved his Hesed banknotes in the Russian's face.

—I should beat you, you filth! Tankilevich shouted.

—Well, well, I'd like to see you try.

But the young mother and her little girl were between them. And the laborer put a restraining hand on the Russian. And the cashier spoke up.

—Be civilized or I will call the police!

And that, more or less, was the end of the spectacle.

His heart still thudding, his groceries sagging in their net bag, Tankilevich left the market and followed the dolorous path to the trolleybus station.

NINE

Normally, Tankilevich called Svetlana from the highway to arrange for her to collect him at the depot. This time he did not call. And when she called, he did not answer. Still, when he descended from the trolleybus and did not immediately see her, he was incensed. With his net bag slapping against his thigh, its weight like razors in his forearm, he staggered from the depot to the road where the cars and taxis were parked. It was evening, but the sun had still to set and he could see clear down the line. He had taken only a few steps before he saw Svetlana striding over to intercept him. Her face, her posture, declared that she had already intuited all.

—She refused you?

—I don't want to discuss it, Tankilevich snapped.

Svetlana reached for the shopping bag and Tankilevich made a play of refusing to yield it.

—Don't be a hero, you look half dead, Svetlana said and took hold of the bag.

They walked in silence back to the car, Svetlana stealing glances at him as they went.

Had there been a single redeeming moment in the entire day? In this one day of a man's life? From dawn to dusk? A single moment? Yes, there had been one. A short distance from the grocery store, when he had stopped to rest his burden, the young mother and her little girl had come alongside him. He expected nothing, averted eyes. But the woman said, *My mother used to work with a Jewish woman, an ophthalmologist. Her husband was a chemist. They were honest, respectable people. Now they live in Israel. How many such valuable people did we lose? Intellectual people. Specialists. Thousands. I don't blame them. Because this country is still primitive, full of primitive people. In front of my daughter, I'm embarrassed for this country.*

There was silence between Svetlana and Tankilevich as she put the groceries in the trunk and he lowered his bulk into the passenger seat. Silence as she veered the car onto the road and began the drive home. Embedded in the silence was his silent command that they remain silent. But he could feel Svetlana straining against the silence and knew that no exercise of his will would keep her quiet long. Abruptly, he turned to face her.

—What do you want me to say? She spat in my face! Tankilevich shouted. That is all.

—I shouldn't have let you go by yourself, Svetlana said, rehashing an old antagonistic line.

—Yes, you should have come with me. This way the trip would have cost double, and, with you along, Nina Semonovna would have simply turned us away at the door.

—Why turned us away? Because I am not Jewish?

—Of course because you are not Jewish! Tankilevich thundered. Don't talk foolishness. It is a *Jewish* organization. One that believes it owes me nothing and you even less.

A large white tour bus had stopped ahead of them. Red letters stenciled on its hull identified it as Polish. Svetlana craned her neck to see what the matter was. Behind them, cars sounded their horns.

—Is he stalled?

Svetlana continued to look and didn't reply.

—Well? Tankilevich persisted.

The bus moved.

—What was it? Tankilevich asked.

They crept along behind the bus but saw no sign of anything amiss. Nothing broken, no one injured on the road. Just indifferent trees and houses on the periphery and the slope of a hill to the east. Nothing out of the ordinary. Nothing to cause a distraction. Nothing at all.

—A day of frustrations. Tankilevich sighed.

It was then that Svetlana told him about the new lodgers. More to crow than to console, Tankilevich felt. As though the lodgers were a flag she was waving in his face. Witness: While he was frittering away his chance in Simferopol, she was securing them lodgers for the week. Lodgers who had paid up front in full. Lodgers who also happened to be Jews. This last, Svetlana delivered with sly significance. Tankilevich didn't miss her implication. That precisely at this moment, these people, being Jews, represented much more than a week's rent. They represented a second chance! Salvation itself!

It was utter childish nonsense, its logic so comprehensively flawed that it pained Tankilevich to think that he was married to a person whose mind wallowed in such inanities.

—Who are these people? he asked bleakly.

—A man and a younger woman, Svetlana replied, bristling at his tone.

—What sort of couple is this?

—Is this our business? They're a couple. They wouldn't be the first such couple.

—Did they say where they were from?

—America.

—But they're Russians?

—Yes. They spoke Russian like you or me.

—And where in Russia are they from?

—That, I didn't ask. If I had to guess, I would say Moscow or St. Petersburg. They didn't strike me as provincial people. Rather, sophisticated people. The man particularly. I would think he would need to be, to get himself such an attractive young companion. Because himself, he is not much to look at. A little nub of a man in a big hat and dark sunglasses. A little Jewish midget, like from a cartoon. Clever, wily. Still, no girl would give herself to such a physically unappealing type if he wasn't wealthy or important.

Tankilevich felt his throat, his entire being, constrict. A tensing against an old pernicious ill. Svetlana, oblivious, looked ready to prattle on, but he cut her off.

—How old would you say is this man?

—How old? I don't know. But I'd give him sixty. Not less.

Gloom, gloom descended on him. That Svetlana had no inkling of it—that she behaved as though enraptured by her own perspicacity and brilliance—astounded him. Tankilevich saw the approach to their house. Svetlana turned the car into the driveway. Night had begun to fall. The house was dark. Dark too were the windows of their Jewish lodgers.

Svetlana opened her door and put a leg out but Tankilevich didn't stir.

—What is it with you? Svetlana asked.

—How is it you have no sense? he said.

—I have no sense? she retorted. What sense is it that I lack?

But when he told her, she waved her hand.

—This is only your paranoia, she said and went to fetch the groceries from the trunk of the car.

Tankilevich made a point of remaining in the car as Svetlana marched to the door with the groceries. She turned once to glance at him over her shoulder, but he stayed obdurately, broodingly in place. She entered the house, and the white rectangles of their rooms flicked consecutively on. In the quiet sanctum of the car, he listened for some soothing intimation.

Svetlana had said *paranoia,* but that was not the right word. It was not paranoid for him to believe that a man such as the one she had described, a Jew of that generation, native to Moscow or Leningrad, part of the intelligentsia, might be able to recognize him. That was no paranoia. That was a fact. A fact that had dictated the course of his life for the past four decades. It had dictated where he could live and whom he could associate with. For those four decades he had taken every precaution to avoid meeting people like the man Svetlana had now recklessly brought into their midst. This was something she knew as well as he. It was the very reason they had met: she had lived in a part of the Soviet Union, the sort of provincial hinterland, where no Jew from Moscow or Leningrad had set foot since collectivization. This was where he had been deposited by the KGB and where he had remained, a Jewish needle in the Soviet haystack, until everything changed and it seemed possible and permissible to venture out. But he and Svetlana had still been guided by the same fact. By then, Yalta seemed as safe as their little Ukrainian hamlet, which was dying a sclerotic death. By then, in Yalta, after the flood of emigration, one was as likely to encounter a Jew from Moscow or Leningrad—now St. Petersburg—as in any rotting kolkhoz. So how was it that something they had registered as a fact, a reality, a peril, something that had accounted for nearly forty years of their lives—how could Svetlana now deride this as paranoia? But after nearly forty years, was the peril the same? Time made specters of perils. But was this true of every peril? And how much time? And who could claim the authority to decide? Who could say to another that his fears were unsubstantiated? That the wolf was not at the door? That the wolf was not even a wolf? And who knew this better than a Jew? Still, he was willing to concede that time had done its work, that time, like water, had eroded the sharpest edges from the peril. What he had feared before—confrontation, outcry, retribution—he did not fear in the same way. Not from a random Russian Jew, even, say, a former activist who might be able to recognize him. Nina Semonovna had spoken of attacks in the press, of newspaper articles, of public excoriation, but he didn't believe that a chance encounter would have the same consequences. And if not those, then what consequences? What was it that he still desperately wished to avoid? Curses? Epithets? Or just that penetrating look of contempt? The tangible evidence that there remained people in the world for whom he was unredeemed, unredeemable.

But had he even this much to fear from the man Svetlana described? This midget with a mistress? What feelings to attribute to this sort of man? No, it was not a case of paranoia that was at issue but a case of overreaction. He and Svetlana both. They were equally at fault. They had each attributed too much to this man. Svetlana had been too hopeful; he too fearful. Hers the exaggerated hope that this man could save them; his the exaggerated fear that this man could harm them.

Back in the house, he sequestered himself in his armchair and watched the insipid programming from Channel One in Moscow. A game show hosted by a facetious impresario. A benevolent *vozhd* who behaved toward the contestants—bumpkins and workers—as if they'd come to touch the hem of his Italian suit. This was what they had raised from the scraps of communism. This was what the struggle for freedom and democracy had delivered. Bread and circuses. Mostly circuses. From one grand deception to another was their lot. First the Soviet sham, then the capitalist. For the ordinary citizen, these were just two different varieties of poison. The current variety served in a nicer bottle.

As Tankilevich allowed the vulgarity to wash over him, Svetlana sat on the sofa with one of the free weekly newspapers on her lap. Occasionally he would hear her rustle a page or sense that she had raised her eyes to glance at the television. Finally she folded her newspaper and stood up. She was almost through the door before she stopped and let out what she had pent up.

—It's not you alone who prays. I also pray. And it may be that God has sent these people to us.

Tankilevich did not even grumble a response but waited for her to leave the room. The game show came to an end and the nightly newscast began. The game show was offensive, but there were no words for the newscast. Every lie starched and ironed. The pomp of a new agreement between Russia and Western corporations to drill for oil in the North Pole. Which everyone knew meant billions of dollars to the same crooks. Condemnation of America for interfering in the affairs of sovereign states. Which meant defending the rights of Arab dictators to shoot their citizens with Russian guns. A clash between authorities and violent demonstrators in Moscow. Which meant the criminal regime stifling dissent. This was Moscow, Russia, and he was in Yalta, Ukraine. But it mattered little. Moscow, Kiev, or Minsk. The same methods prevailed.

Tankilevich turned off the television and rose heavily to his feet. He was overcome by fatigue. The fatigue of living in this country. The fatigue of enduring a day of such indignities—after a life of such indignities. He took a few steps and then caught his haggard reflection in the window. There had been a time when women considered him handsome and he had prided himself on his looks. Now he was like an old elephant, a big gray beast sagging to the earth. He ran his hand through his hair and cleared his throat. More quaveringly than he intended, he called to Svetlana.

—Mother, if you're not praying, make some tea.

Reunion

TEN

At dawn Kotler opened his eyes. He had been lying in bed for what seemed like hours with his eyes shut, thinking, thinking. For part of this time, he had heard Leora shifting beside him. Then she had grown still, her breathing become that of a sleeping person. He wished to sleep too, but his mind was too active. For a man of his vocation—civic life, politics—sleepless nights should not have been uncommon. Indeed, for months now he had been embroiled in a political struggle and a love affair, but he could not say that he had lost an entire night's sleep. An hour here or there, certainly, but not a full night watching the chromatic spool in his head. In fact, part of what kept him awake were recollections of sleepless nights past. The sleepless nights after Tankilevich's article ran in *Izvestia*. That article had marked the beginning of his third life. First life: rank-and-file Soviet citizen. Second life: rank-and-file dissident. Third life: the chosen among the chosen. Many sleepless nights followed: sleepless nights waiting for the knock on the door; sleepless nights in his cell in Lefortovo, parsing his interrogator's every word and gesture, trying to squirm his way out of the psychological maze; sleepless nights during his trial, chiseling away at the lies of his accusers; sleepless nights in solitary confinement, in conditions too brutish for sleep; and sleepless nights in the camps before a hunger strike, steeling himself for the ordeal, incanting a Hebrew phrase he had memorized, the words ringing like hammer blows: *Justice, justice, shall you pursue.*

And now what was he pursuing? Kotler asked himself. *Justice, justice,* he playfully replied.

He swung his legs around and rose from the bed. He pulled on his trousers and his shirt. Barefoot, he padded to the window. The chickens were out, pecking. *Ma nishma,* chickens? he greeted them. Joviality in the face of adversity, that was the secret of his success. And of my undoing! he appended to himself jovially.

Behind him, Leora stirred. He turned from the window. This was how they had spent their first, and possibly last, night alone together. Lying silently in the same bed, thinking their separate, divergent thoughts. Very like a married couple. Another of life's scintillating ironies.

Leora slowly opened her eyes. How lovely she looked, even when she awoke cross. He smiled at her and told her so.

—What time is it, Baruch?

Kotler consulted his wristwatch.

—Early. Just past six.

—Did you sleep?

—I thought about it.

Leora sat up and brushed the sheets aside. She wore her brassiere and panties. He had worn his underpants. The stuff of bourgeoisie comedy.

—You haven't changed your mind? Leora asked.

—Many times, Kotler said. But it always changed back.

She stood up and surveyed the room. Her dress lay on the floor beside the chair. She moved to pick it up. Kotler watched with admiration and longing—the longing for a thing that is slipping from one's grasp—as she raised her arms and the dress slid down the length of her body. The closing curtain on a fine spectacle.

—All right, then, what do you intend to do?

Kotler looked at his watch again, as if he hadn't looked at it a minute before.

—If I knew where we could get one, I would like to see a newspaper. A cup of coffee would be nice too.

—Very well, Leora said and took a determined step toward the door.

—There's no need for that, Leora, Kotler said.

—No need for what? If you wish to do this, why delay? I'll wake the lady of the house. I'll ask her for a newspaper and a cup of coffee. And then we can get to the business at hand. The sooner we start, the sooner we'll finish. Or isn't that the point?

—That probably is the point. As usual, you're more astute than I. I had visions of something grand and involved, but likely it will be nothing of the kind. As is often the case in life, one imagines an opera and gets an operetta. If that. Still, I'd prefer to do this in a civilized manner. No banging on doors. No rousing from sleep. The time for that is past.

—From what I have seen, Baruch, the time for that is not past.

—Even so. Let's behave as if it is and wait for the world to follow our noble example.

—None of this is even remotely funny to me.

—No, I know it isn't, Kotler said.

Leora looked at him from where she had stalled, partway to the door.

—Would you like to hear about the last time I shared a roof with this man? Kotler asked. You've said more than once that you were interested in the stories of the glorious past. So here is one I've never told you. It's one I've hardly spoken of at all, as far as I can remember. Perhaps to a few cellmates and to Miriam. Because it isn't much of a story. It's the opposite. A nonstory. Even in my memoir, my editor chose to edit it out. But it is the story of the last night I spent under the same roof with Vladimir Tankilevich.

Leora sighed and walked slowly back to the bed. She sat on its edge and looked at Kotler like someone submitting reluctantly to the sway of a hypnotist. Kotler, who remained near the window, would have liked to sit beside her as in times past, but refrained. Times past now included the previous day, the previous hour. He was responsible for it. He still had the power to change it. But he knew he would not. A man could not live two lives. A man was condemned to choose and he had chosen.

—Fine, Baruch, tell me. Tell me so that we can get on with things.

There was his gospel, the substance of which Leora knew, as, once, did millions of others. A young man, a lapsed musician turned computer scientist, embraces his Jewish identity and resolves to quit the Soviet Union for Israel, his ancestral homeland. His application for an exit visa is routinely, arbitrarily denied by the Interior Ministry for unsubstantiated "security reasons"—even though he possesses no technical knowledge that isn't already old news in the West. He is branded a traitor, fired from his job, designated a criminal—since it is a crime to be without work in the workers' state. He falls in love with a young woman, also a Zionist; they marry quickly in the hope that this will bind their fates but are nonetheless separated when she, just as arbitrarily, is permitted to leave and he, again, is not. While he waits to join her, he throws himself into activist work and is framed by a fellow Jew, a KGB plant. Charged with treason, subjected to a show trial, he is sentenced to death, but then, after an international outcry, he is locked up for thirteen years instead of being shot in the head. All the while, he resists, resists, resists! Until finally, triumphantly, he is released.

But there was more, of course. The minor notes and episodes, less spectacular but, for him, more consuming. His final night in the apartment he shared with Tankilevich represented one. For until Tankilevich took him in, he had been homeless. Miriam had left for Israel. Their small apartment had been registered in her name, and once she departed—for it was virtually a rule among refuseniks that nobody should forfeit the chance to go—he had to move out. With no job and no apartment, he slept, a week here and a week there, in the homes of other refuseniks and of sympathizers. Everything he owned he carried in a small suitcase. The man who would soon become the world's most illustrious refusenik was a pauper whose belongings would have been declined by a junk shop. And then, at no small personal risk, Tankilevich offered to take him in. A marginal character in Kotler's life before then, Tankilevich had appeared in their midst a year earlier. He presented himself as a Zionist and declared he had been refused an exit visa—nobody bothered to verify. If KGB spies had infiltrated their ranks, there wasn't much they could do about it. In any case, everything they did—the Hebrew classes, the Passover seders, their small public demonstrations—was technically legal.

They made an odd pairing, the two of them. Tankilevich was almost a decade older, a bachelor, impressive-looking, while Kotler was a balding, feisty little schmendrik. By trade, Tankilevich was a dental technician, and he volunteered his services to other refuseniks, making dentures, caps, and crowns. Since he was ostensibly under refusal, he could not work officially. Everyone understood the implications: How could a refusenik handle gold and silver? He was susceptible to a charge of commercialism or speculation. This was grounds for suspicion. People discussed this, and Chava Margolis, as usual, staked out the most skeptical position—even though she too had one of Tankilevich's bridges in her mouth.

But Kotler never found any reason to distrust him and came to consider him a friend, a confidant. He was nursing the pain of Miriam's departure. Sometimes the two men sat together and listened to classical music: Scriabin, Prokofiev, Shostakovich. They studied Jewish subjects and practiced their clumsy Hebrew. There was nothing out of the ordinary until the night before Tankilevich's denunciation ran in *Izvestia*.

And what of that night? Kotler was in the apartment, writing a press release for Western outlets about the conditions inside the psychiatric hospitals. They'd received sworn affidavits from a dissident who had emerged from one and, remarkably, from a psychiatric nurse who was appalled by what she had seen—taking sane, healthy people, confining them with lunatics, and injecting them with drugs until they became like lunatics themselves. Kotler was composing his text at a table in the front room when Tankilevich came home. They exchanged the usual greetings. *Shalom. Shalom.* Everything as always. Tankilevich asked what he was doing. Kotler told him. Tankilevich considered attentively and then excused himself, going into the kitchen. Kotler continued his work. Then, suddenly, there was a crash, a sound of breaking plates. Not just one or two; it was as though every plate in the kitchen had been dashed. Kotler sprang up from the table and found Tankilevich standing amid the shards of an entire stack of dinner plates. With a very peculiar expression on his face. Not startled or agitated or regretful. Rather, detached. As if he was mildly, distantly intrigued by the mess around him. *Volodya, what happened?* Kotler said. *Nothing, a trifle* came the answer. Kotler offered to get a broom, to sweep up. But Tankilevich said, *No need, I'll do it.* Because he was behaving so strangely, Kotler didn't insist. He let him be. They were all under a great deal of stress and nobody knew all that weighed on another man's heart. Kotler went back to work. He heard Tankilevich sweeping. Then some fumbling and shuffling that he couldn't identify. He expected Tankilevich to go to the corridor and toss the broken things into the dustbin, but when he looked in on him, he found him at the kitchen table gluing the pieces back together. How many plates had been broken? Ten? Twelve? There was a considerable jumble. The plates themselves were nothing special, neither heirlooms nor imports. They were the most ordinary Soviet plates and could be purchased in any store for fifty kopeks apiece. To replace them would have been easy. There were deficits and shortages of practically everything then, but not of those sorts of things. So why go to the trouble? *Volodya, what are you doing that for?* he asked. To which Tankilevich replied, *It calms the soul.*

Those were the last civil words they exchanged. Period. The end.

Leora listened to all this dully, with neither expression nor reaction.

—And the mystery? she asked.

—You see, I told you it wasn't much of a story.

—I just don't see the mystery.

—The mystery? The entire thing. Did he dash the plates deliberately or did they fall by accident? And what was going through his head?

—Of course he dashed them, Baruch.

—Yes? And what was going through his head?

—He was conflicted. Stricken by conscience. He didn't want to face you.

—There's that.

—What else could there be?

—I don't know. But life has taught me that there is always something else. Some surprise beyond the scope of my limited imagination.

Through the door they heard movement, the sounds of the day's first activities, a kettle set on a burner.

—Well, Leora said, here is your chance to find out.

She rose from the bed and walked briskly to the door. This time Kotler did not inhibit her. She opened the door and passed into the hall. The sounds of a morning's preparations came more distinctly now. He heard Leora greeting their landlady and the woman returning the greeting and inquiring if Leora would be having breakfast. There was also the sound of a man's grumbled *Good morning.* Kotler felt a jolt in his heart. And yet, if he hadn't already known that this voice belonged to Tankilevich, would he have recognized it?

Here it was. The moment he had fantasized about had finally arrived. Naturally, it was not how he'd envisioned it. In his vanity, he had always imagined meeting Tankilevich and his other former tormentors at the height of his powers, when he could gaze down upon them like a Zeus upon mortals. But this wasn't how things stood now. It could be said that he was now as low as he had ever been and that he could not have chosen a less auspicious time for this grand reunion. But now was when it had happened. Only a fool believed that the world was built to stoke his vanity. Not from the heights but from the depths was life truly lived! And other such *hokhmes.*

Forward! Kotler commanded himself.

Ten strides and he was in the kitchen, facing his audience. He found the women on their feet and Tankilevich at the kitchen table, a teacup between his hands. That Leora eyed him expectantly was no surprise. But he saw similar expressions on the faces of Svetlana and Tankilevich. As if they too had been intent upon his appearance. What had they been expecting? Clearly not him. Tankilevich flinched and knocked his teacup against its saucer. He looked down to see if the liquid had spilled but when he looked up, his face had hardened and set. There was no doubt. No doubt for either of them.

—*Boker tov,* Volodya, Kotler said.

Like quicksilver, a look flashed between Tankilevich and his wife. Kotler saw the woman's face blanch. Instinctively, she crossed herself.

—My God, she said.

—Your God, Tankilevich snapped. See how He's answered your prayers.

He turned from his wife and glared at Kotler with the loathing of a cornered animal.

—A merry game, eh? An important man like you, you've got nothing better to do? Well, have a good look around, then. Here's your old enemy. The despicable beast. The disgrace of the Jewish people. See how fate has settled its accounts with him. Give your girl a good laugh at his expense.

—What do you think, Volodya, Kotler said, that I had the Mossad hunt you down? That we chased you fifteen years, like Eichmann?

—You've come to insult me? Insult me. Rejoice. I'm a defenseless man. Say what you want and leave us be.

—Volodya, it's pure coincidence, not the Mossad, that has brought me here. I've no more sought you than you've sought me.

—Chaim, Tankilevich said.

—What's that? Kotler asked.

—I go by Chaim, Tankilevich said resolutely.

—Ah, you see, Leora, Kotler said with a grin, the first surprise.

—What's the surprise? Tankilevich demanded. You alone reserve the right to change your name? I'm no less a Jew than you. No less a Zionist either.

—I'm glad to hear it, Kotler said. Though, if you'll forgive my saying so, this also comes as a surprise. The last time I saw you, you denounced me before a Soviet tribunal as a Zionist imperialist spy working for the American intelligence services.

Splaying his hands on the tabletop, Tankilevich pushed back

his chair and rose stiffly. He cast another baleful look at his wife and then turned to face Kotler.

—What do you want? You have come to collect? Well, I have paid and paid for my sins. I have paid in excess. I am paying still. And I have nothing for you.

On his way out of the kitchen, Tankilevich glanced one last time at his wife.

—Return their money.

The three of them watched his broad back fill the doorway and listened to his ponderous steps in the corridor. There was the sound of the front door opening and closing, and of footfalls on the gravel outside.

After an instant, recovering from her shocked state, Svetlana sprang from the table and went in pursuit of her husband, leaving Kotler and Leora to each other. The door opened and slammed shut again, and Svetlana's footfalls joined her husband's on the gravel path. From Leora came the unspoken question: *Satisfied?* To which what could Kotler reply? *In a way.*

Through the kitchen window it was possible to see what was unfolding in the driveway. Svetlana caught up to Tankilevich as he unlocked the car door and was preparing to lower himself into the driver's seat. She gripped the door and would not release it. Kotler and Leora watched the struggle between them and heard the more heated parts of their argument.

From Svetlana: *With your eyes! Have you forgotten what the doctor said? Suicide!*

And from Tankilevich: *I want those people out of my house!*

The standoff continued for a little longer. Tankilevich resisted and did not easily relinquish the wheel, but Svetlana held fast and wouldn't allow him to close the door. Eventually, in supreme frustration, Tankilevich wrenched himself from the car and stalked off toward the road. In parting he declared: *One hour!*

Svetlana watched him go, and when he had disappeared from view, she eased shut the car door. She then looked back to the house, where she found Kotler and Leora at the kitchen window. She eyed them grimly, then started inside. Before long, she was back in the kitchen. Nobody spoke and the room felt hollowed out, vacuous. The three of them regarded one another as through spans of chilled space. Svetlana, looking sorely perplexed, broke the silence.

—Is what my husband said true?

—What part? Kotler replied.

—That you came here deliberately.

—You were at the bus station. Do you believe we staged that encounter? Does that seem plausible to you?

—I don't care about plausible. I am asking you if it is true.

—Svetlana, ask yourself: If we knew where to find you, why would we even bother with such contortions? Why would we not come straight to your door?

—So you deny it?

—I've already denied it. I denied it to your husband. I can deny it a thousand more times. But to what end? In my experience, denial is pointless. It is just words. What matters is logic and proof. I see you are not a simple woman. Ask yourself a different question: *Why* would I deny this? If indeed I sought your husband out, why wouldn't I say so? Why would I engage in this pretense? Especially since, as anyone will tell you, I am a terrible actor. My strength, such as it is, lies in the opposite direction.

Svetlana stopped to consider this, to consider him. Kotler felt as though he could discern, behind her eyes, the minutest cogitations of her mind. He saw her reach a decision, the thought clicking into place. She turned to the stove and lifted the kettle, which had just started to whistle. Kettle in hand, she faced Kotler and Leora.

—You will have some tea? she inquired. Or coffee?

—It's very hospitable of you, Kotler said, but perhaps unwise. Your husband doesn't want us here and we've no interest in imposing ourselves.

Svetlana strode to the table and dismissed Kotler's reservations with a wave of her hand. She put the kettle down.

—My husband does not alone decide. Please sit. There will be plenty of time to leave. Besides, where would you go now? It is not even seven o'clock. Where would you find a room at this hour? And without even so much as a bite to eat? I would not allow it.

—We are perfectly capable of fending for ourselves, Leora said.

—Who says you are not? But you are in our house. You are our guests. By Divine Providence, if what you say is true. Never mind my husband. I have my own convictions, Christian convictions, if I can say such a thing in front of you.

—Why not? Kotler said. We are not offended by Christian convictions. Particularly if they lead to nothing worse than a cup of coffee.

—Good, then, Svetlana said. You'll sit.

She went to a cupboard, opened its door, and retrieved a jar of instant coffee. As she did so, Kotler lowered himself into one of the kitchen chairs. He looked to Leora to follow suit, but she held her ground with a tired obstinacy. Passive resistance. *Fine, but for what sake?* Kotler wordlessly inquired. *Just so. For no sake,* came Leora's wordless reply.

Holding the jar of coffee in her hand, Svetlana observed the two of them.

—You won't sit? she asked Leora, in a tone both anxious and reproachful.

—She is registering her disapproval, Kotler said.

—Of what does she disapprove?

—Of remaining here.

—Of coming here in the first place, Leora calmly corrected.

—But if fate brought you here, how can you disapprove? Svetlana said.

—It turns out, very easily.

—But what is the point of disapproving? If it is fate, your disapproval will not change it. Standing instead of sitting in my kitchen will not change it. Even walking out the door will not change it. A tree will fall across your path. Because if fate has ordained to bring you here, it will conspire to keep you here. I am older than you. I have lived a life. What I say I say from experience. One needs time on this earth to understand fate.

Svetlana turned to Kotler and asked: Is it not so?

—I would say that one walks hand in hand with fate. Fate pulls in one direction, you pull in the other. You follow fate; fate follows you. And it is not always possible to say who is leading whom.

—But you say fate led you here.

—Fate led; I followed. I chose to follow. At first innocently, obliviously. But once I recognized where fate was leading me, no longer obliviously. Then I chose with full and deliberate knowledge. Leora would have preferred if I had chosen differently.

Svetlana went to the table and placed the coffee jar beside the kettle. She looked again at Leora.

—Will you also take coffee? Because if you will, I would ask that you sit. Even if you won't take coffee, I would ask that you sit. I find your standing very disconcerting. It grates on my nerves. It is like having a policeman or an undertaker in the house.

Leora inhaled dramatically and, with slow leisurely strides, crossed the room and took a seat opposite Kotler. She looked up at Svetlana and made a little theatrical gesture with her hands. A gesture of *There, I have complied.*

—Will you take coffee? Svetlana asked her.

—After all that, how could I not?

Svetlana poured the hot water into three teacups. Then came the ceremony with the teaspoons and the stirring and mixing. She passed Kotler and Leora each a cup and took her seat between them. They all observed a brief, tactical lull while they sipped their drinks.

—If I may, Kotler offered, you mentioned your Christian convictions. I'm interested to know what you meant.

—I believe in God's grace. I believe that He hears our prayers.

—Which would make us the answer to those prayers?

—How would you explain your arrival here?

—May I ask what you prayed for?

—Like everyone else, Svetlana said, I prayed for His mercy. I prayed for Him to ease the burden of our suffering.

—If that's the case, it would seem He sent you the most unlikely emissaries.

—Isn't that how we recognize His hand?

—And how do you know it is your prayer He is answering?

—Who else's? Yours? Hers?

—Certainly not mine, Leora said.

—Yours, then? Svetlana inquired. Are you a believer?

—Not like that, Kotler said. It's many years since I prayed. But who knows how long it takes a prayer to reach God's ears? And how long for Him to respond? When I was in prison, I asked Him to grant me the satisfaction of facing my tormentors as a free man. That was a long time ago. But perhaps a prayer is like a radio signal, flying through space until it finds its mark. And the answer arrives not when you want it but when it suits God, when you have long since stopped waiting for it.

—Well, what is to say He hasn't answered both our prayers?

—I think that would be quite a feat, even for God.

The trill of Kotler's cell phone sounded. He fished the device out of his pocket and inspected the name on the screen.

—It's my son, Kotler said. Excuse me.

He rose from the table and took two steps before he brought the phone to his ear. He spoke his son's name and heard his voice in reply. In the background, he heard also the grinding sounds of heavy machinery, the rumble of diesel engines, and the clatter of a half-track.

—One moment, Benzka, Kotler said. Let me just—

He went into his and Leora's room and closed the door. He gravitated to the window and looked out at the familiarly uneventful yard. So unlike the scene he pictured surrounding his young son. The word *young* interposed itself. They had tasked young men—somber children with long limbs and smooth cheeks—to undertake this ugly job. To smash the work of their brothers and expel the brothers too. To do it and continue to believe that, afterward, they could still be brothers. And to trust that this served the greater good. A good for all: the enforcer and the resister, and the nation of onlookers who sat wringing their hands in front of their televisions. *Vey iz mir,* as his father would have said. Where were they headed?

—I was going to call you, Kotler said. I was waiting until seven.

—They are moving us now. A few of the guys are still davening *shacharit*. But they can only drag it out for so long before the commanders say, *Enough.*

—A busy day for God. So many prayers to answer.

—Not so many, Benzion said. Not enough.

—How are you, Benzka? Kotler asked with fatherly inflection.

—Don't say it like that, Benzion said. That isn't why I called. I don't want to talk about that.

Benzion's voice faltered and Kotler felt the same impulse he had had when his son was small and someone had caused him pain. The innate desire to console. But his son was no longer small and didn't want to be consoled. Besides, this time Kotler was the one who had caused him pain. So what use was his sympathy?

—I talked with Rabbi Gedalia and I talked with some of the guys, Benzion proceeded. We don't want to do it.

—I understand, Benzion. It's a terrible thing that is being asked of you boys. I wish with all my heart that it hadn't come to this. But are you calling to inform me of your decision or to ask my opinion?

—Tell me why I should do it.

—I have no inspired answer to this. You're a soldier in our nation's army. The answer I'll give will be the same as the one you get from your commanders and the minister of defense. However much I disagree with him about this operation, I don't disagree that a soldier's job is to obey orders.

—Even immoral orders?

—No, not immoral orders. But it says nothing in the Geneva Conventions about dismantling your own settlements.

—It says it in the Torah.

—I'm not so sure it says it in the Torah either. But you know I'm no Torah scholar. Anyway, that's neither here nor there. Like it or not, our country is a democracy. The Torah is very nice, but we don't run the country by it. If we ever did.

—Rabbi Gedalia says different.

—I'm sure he does.

—So do many other people.

—Well, if you have a majority, you can form the next government.

—So that's it? You're saying I should go along with this even if it makes me sick? Even if I believe with perfect faith that it is wrong, a sin against God to give up our land? You can tell me honestly that this is what you would do?

—Benzka, if you have called for my blessing, I can't give it. I would like to give it. After what has happened and after what I have done, I want nothing more than to give you what you want. But as much as I love you, and as much as I want to please you, I can't lie to you, my son. Because I love you, I can't lie to you.

—You lied already.

—There are lies and there are lies.

—You say.

—This is your father, imperfect.

—So that's all?

—You ask what I would do in your place. Let me ask you. What would happen to our army and our country if soldiers started to choose what orders they would follow? One believes evicting settlers is wrong, another believes the occupation is illegal.

—So instead we should all go against our consciences and wait until the next election? Is this what you did in the Soviet Union?

—Despite what some people say, the time has not yet come to compare Israel to the Soviet Union.

—I'm not talking about that. I'm talking about a person's soul. When it screams, *No*. What are you supposed to do? Ignore it? If you see that your country is on the road to ruin, do you not do something about it? Before it's too late.

—This is what you believe?

—It's what you yourself said.

—As a politician, not a soldier. And not exactly for the same reasons.

—I don't see a big difference.

—So then what can I say, Benzka? You'll do as you see fit.

—And you won't support me?

—If you disobey orders, no. I'm sorry.

—But I'm telling you I have no choice.

—That's not true. If you think there's no choice, look harder. There is always a choice. A third way, if not a fourth. Whether we have the strength to make those choices is another matter. Of which I am no less guilty than anyone else.

ELEVEN

Leora and Svetlana looked down the corridor to where Kotler had disappeared. They kept their eyes fixed on the spot past the point of all discomfort. They were now trapped together without a word to say. Leora laced her fingers around her teacup and looked anywhere but at Svetlana. If necessary, she could sit like this for hours, for as long as it took. How many times had she sat in some government office or waiting room waging a silent war with a receptionist or rival aide? How many times during the last round of negotiations had she been sequestered with the junior members of the Palestinian delegation staring at the closed door behind which the fruitless talks were being conducted?

She had grown up waiting. She had watched her parents wait. Righteous, implacable, and unheralded. They were modest heroes, nothing like Kotler and Miriam and the others whose names had made it into the newspapers. But they had waited no less honorably. And from their example Leora had learned her first and most instructive lesson. The iron lesson: *We will out-*

wait them. The lesson that had sustained and defined the Jews for thousands of years. It now also sustained and defined their enemies. Both parties, masters of waiting. Across the table and across the fence, waiting each other into oblivion.

Svetlana shifted in her seat and pushed back her chair. Out of the corner of her eye, Leora watched the woman until she left the room. Unwilling to turn her head, she continued to gaze at nothing and to strain her ears. She tried to decipher even a single word of Kotler's telephone conversation but heard only Svetlana's steps moving across the floor and receding up the hall. Then a door creaking on its hinges followed by more of Svetlana's heavy, muffled steps. After that came finer sounds: the sliding of a wooden drawer; the snapping of a clasp; some papery rustling. Finally, the repetition of all these sounds in reverse, until Svetlana was again in the kitchen, standing before Leora with her arm extended, a fold of bills in her palm.

—It's all here, Svetlana said. I didn't deduct for last night.

—That's your prerogative, Leora said. But the money is Baruch's, not mine. You can give it to him.

—But you see the money is already in my hand. I give it to you or I give it to him, what's the difference?

—I told you the difference. The money is his. Give it to him. It's not for me to accept.

Svetlana looked at the money as if it were now the crux of a thorny dilemma. She resolved it by turning her palm over and laying the money on the tabletop. She resumed her seat and silence reigned between them again. Though this time Svetlana looked directly at Leora, studied her plainly and knowingly.

—I understand, I understand, Svetlana said. You dislike me. You hold an opinion of me. In your eyes, I am a certain kind of woman. A disreputable woman. Because what other kind of woman would marry a man like my husband?

—To be honest, Leora said, I haven't given much thought to you or your character. You and your character matter very little to me. At the risk of insulting you, you and your character are at the very bottom of the list of my concerns. If that.

—Yes, and what are your concerns? Svetlana inquired, undeterred.

—Please, let's just sit here quietly until Baruch returns. Or if you absolutely must speak, let's talk about the weather or your recipe for borscht.

—You believe you are very different from me, but you are mistaken. I was also a young girl who fell for an older, worldly man. A man who seemed unlike other men. The others drank, strutted, talked foolishness. You knew what your life would be like if you bound yourself to them. But then a man appears who seems to be lit from within. Yes? How else to describe it? When you look at him, you see the glow. And you think that only he can rescue you from the bleak life that is inundating you like a flood.

Svetlana leaned toward Leora. *Isn't that so?* she asked, to which Leora didn't reply. What could she say to her? She detested such talk. This psychoanalyzing. The sort of idiotic conversation that passed for revelation over white wine in Tel Aviv.

—I don't know what you think you know about our lives, Svetlana pressed on. Let me ask you, where were you born?

Leora had no wish to swap biographical data, but Svetlana waited for her answer nonetheless.

—Moscow, Leora finally said.

—And how long did you live there?

—When I was six, we left.

—Consider yourself a lucky person.

—I have no regrets. But I've seen places worse than Russia and Ukraine. There are even people who've left Israel and moved back here. I can tell you, the Ethiopians who come to Israel don't do that.

—What do they move back here for?

—For an easier life. Why else do people move?

—Really? I'd very much like to see this easier life. I have two daughters, both educated, with no prospects. I have a son-in-law sitting idle in Simferopol. For three months he was a policeman in Yalta. In a narcotics unit. Would you like to know what that means?

—Very much, Leora said.

—Good, I'll tell you, Svetlana said, parrying Leora's sarcasm. His salary was one hundred and fifty dollars a month. They also gave him a police car and ten dollars a month for gas. Ten dollars for gas was good for one day. The rest had to come from his pocket. The cost of notebooks and pens to write the reports—his pocket. Money to buy drugs from the criminals so as to catch them—his pocket. Now, how did they expect a person to survive like this? Could a policeman do his job faithfully? Either a person becomes corrupt or he abandons this job. Most of them become corrupt. Ours said he didn't have the constitution for it. It didn't agree with him to work in such an environment. So he resigned. Is it better for his constitution to live without regular work in Simferopol?

Svetlana looked pointedly at Leora, as if she expected her rebuttal.

—I don't know what you want me to say.

—There's nothing to say, Svetlana declared. Only one time in my life did I allow myself to feel hopeful in this country, and that was when I met Chaim. I was twenty years old and I lived in a village that could fit inside Yalta fifty times over. He appeared at the regional dental clinic. I couldn't imagine what would have brought him to such a provincial place, but it was Soviet times and a person was like a pebble in the hand of the regime, tossed here or there. Or if someone wanted to shed his old life, there were a million villages from Kamchatka to Baku. All I knew of my husband was that he had been born in Chernovets, spent the war in Kazakhstan, and later lived in Moscow. The man I married was named Vladimir Tarasov. His passport said his nationality was Russian. We were married in 1979. It was only ten years later, when the Soviet Union was on its last legs, that I learned the truth. By this time we had our two daughters, and life in the village was becoming intolerable. People were being paid their salaries in vodka. A truck would pull up and they would hand out bottles. Can you imagine? Not just to the laborers but also to the schoolteachers. And it was only when I insisted that we leave the village that he told me his secret. He wept.

—Not from contrition, I suppose.

—It is easy to judge, Svetlana said. But he was a man who had hidden his true self for over a decade. From the people closest to him. From his very children. Do you think it is easy?

—It depends what you are hiding. All husbands hide things from their wives, and all parents hide things from their children. I'm surprised he chose to confess such a thing at all.

—Such a thing? It was his essence.

—That he was a KGB informant?

—That he was a Jew.

—He wouldn't have been the first to conceal that inconvenient fact either. Unless it was no longer inconvenient. A lot of people discovered their Jewish ancestry at this time. You can see them on Sundays at the Church of the Holy Sepulchre.

—Have you seen him at the Church of the Holy Sepulchre? Have you seen either of us? Though, I won't lie, I would dearly love to go. I would like to go to the Church of the Holy Sepulchre almost as much as he would like to go to the Wailing Wall.

—Very well. Go. Who's stopping you? It's a free country. Jerusalem is full of pilgrims. Not a few of them Russians. At the Jaffa Gate they are disgorged by the busload. Every third word in the souk is Russian. Even the Arab storekeepers speak it now.

—Very nice, but it isn't about being a pilgrim.

—No? Then what is it about?

—You heard him. He's a Zionist. He wants to live in Israel.

—Fine. So go. *B'hatzlacha.* I'm not going to stop you. Neither is Baruch, I suspect.

—But you know we cannot do that. After what my husband did, he will never be accepted. Nor will our daughters.

—I don't know anything of the sort. You should see some of the people we've accepted. The Law of Return doesn't discriminate. Or not enough. Even against gangsters and traitors.

—I am not talking about legally.

—No? Then how?

—Spiritually. How can a person live in a country where his name is despised?

—Your husband should have asked himself that question forty years ago.

—Believe me, my dear, he asked it.

—And apparently answered it.

Leora watched Svetlana run a hand across her forehead, as in frustration and sorrow.

—Oh, girl, how easy it is to sit in judgment when one doesn't hold all the facts.

And just when Leora had thought she couldn't feel more distaste for this woman, with her unctuous, melodramatic, wheedling tone. Leora stole another glance down the hallway in hopes that Baruch would emerge. How much more could she possibly say to this woman? Were they to have an esoteric conversation about justice? Who is the real victim? Who is the real perpetrator? Who gets to sit in judgment? *Who?* Everyone. And only a child or a simpleton bemoans it. To sit in judgment without all the facts? Who ever sat in judgment *with* all the facts? Facts were imposed by those who had the power to impose them. Today, it suited the newspapers to depict her as a wide-eyed, impressionable fawn. Tomorrow, different facts would paint her as a sly, self-seeking tart. And later still, depending on the way the winds were blowing, she could find herself on a soundstage in intimate conversation with a television host, with the furniture, the coffee mugs, and the pretensions of compassion and sincerity. But neither in that setting nor in this kitchen could Leora imagine speaking candidly about herself and Baruch. None of them deserved to hear it. The world was full of jackals; they ravaged your life, and there was little you could keep from them except a few small tokens of introspection:

Her earliest girlhood in the Moscow apartment. Returning in tears from kindergarten and the playground to the firm inculcations of her father. *Never be ashamed. Hold your head high. You are the daughter of a proud and ancient people.*

Her parents' gallery of heroes, some of whom passed through their doors, others imprisoned, their photographs cut from newspapers and kept in a scrapbook. Baruch's photograph among them, given pride of place. Though by the time she was old enough to comprehend, he had gained his release. Different photos depicted this triumph. The small rumpled man with the mischievous grin saluting the honor guard at Ben Gurion Airport. Listening as the prime minister bent close to speak into his ear. Carried aloft on the shoulders of an exultant crowd. Facing a bank of lights and microphones, holding the hand of the pretty, patient wife.

The scrapbook and the walnut armoire in which it was kept went with them to Petah Tikva. But in Israel there was no longer a need for the pictures. The Soviet foe had been vanquished, that battle had been won. Replaced by the new battle—to carve out a life in the Promised Land. After school, alone in the apartment, awaiting her parents' return, she sometimes paged through the book, whose radiance was slowest to dim for a child.

The anniversary of Jerusalem Day, attending with her parents a gathering of former refuseniks in Ben Shemen Forest. The picnic tables under the pines. The flags strung between the tree trunks. The old activists, gone gray, but their energy undiminished. Like her parents, they came with children, grandchildren. For most, the anniversary was coincident with the anniversary of their national revival. In a manner of speaking, the Israeli paratroopers who had liberated Jerusalem had also liberated them. Here she had met Baruch for the first time. A microphone, an electric keyboard, and an amplifier were plugged into the battery of a Volkswagen. Baruch stood at the keyboard and, with an accordionist and her own father on guitar, provided accompaniment for a rendition of "Kachol Velavan." Afterward, her father introduced her. She was twenty-two, in her final year of university. *A serious girl. A serious student,* her father said proudly. *I can see,* Baruch teased and then asked about her plans. *I'm interested in politics,* she found the courage to say. *You've raised an activist, Yitzhak,* Baruch said. *There are worse things,* her father replied. *Not according to* my *daughter!* countered Baruch with a grin.

And the winter trade mission to Helsinki. The tours of the mobile-phone factories and paper mills. Baruch outfitted against the cold in a fashionable coat that she and Dafna had bought for him at the Mamilla shopping mall. *People will mistake me for an Austrian ski racer,* he'd protested. His existing winter coat dated from 1992, bought at a Kiev market on the occasion of his symbolic return to the former Soviet Union. Maybe acceptable for a Ukrainian transport worker but unfit, Dafna and Leora had pronounced, for the Israeli minister of trade. Seeing him in the coat was a constant reminder to Leora of her afternoon with Dafna, wandering the shops, drinking cappuccinos at the Aroma Café. Like two girlfriends. And in the hotel room, though the coat was stowed in the closet, discreetly out of sight, she nevertheless felt its reproving presence, as though it bore silent witness to what she and Baruch were doing in the bed. Neither of them was rich in experience, but he made her feel the more practiced, the more assured. He wrapped his arms around her chest, pressed his face against her back, and sat still as a statue, as though drawing sustenance. And in the moment of climax, he called out as if in gratitude, as if she had alleviated some ache.

To whom could she confide such things?

To Svetlana, she said, So you think God sent us here for your redemption. To shepherd you into the Holy Land. With Baruch the shepherd and your husband the lamb.

—Do you believe in God? Svetlana asked.

—What does it matter?

—If we are going to speak of God, it matters. I need to know what kind of person I am speaking with. One who believes or one who doesn't. It isn't the same conversation. And if you believe, you will know this.

—Then say I believe.

—Then I will repeat myself. I believe in the grace of our Lord. I believe in His justice and mercy. If you say you believe, then I take it you agree. Or what sort of God is there to believe in? A sadist who only metes out suffering?

—He does that too.

—He punishes the sinner according to his sin. But He also forgives. And He rewards the true penitent. Don't we also believe this? That when we transgress we can seek His forgiveness?

—So your husband has repented and is deserving of forgiveness.

—My husband has repented a hundred times over. For decades he has borne his punishment. But he is not the worst of men. Far from it. Whether you believe it or not. What he did forty years ago, he did with a heavy heart. What he did, he did against his conscience. And he has suffered for it in more ways than I can say.

—Is it still God's mercy we're talking about?

—For me, God's mercy is no longer the question. I know He

is merciful. Not just on faith. I know it because I see the evidence of His mercy.

At this, Svetlana fixed her eyes on Leora with a fervent, meaningful conviction. The gaze of a holy communicant.

—That He brought you to us now is a sign of His mercy. That is how I see it, Svetlana said. So it is no longer about His mercy.

—It isn't? Then whose? Leora asked, incorrectly anticipating the answer.

—Yours, of course.

—Mine? Leora asked. You don't mean mine specifically?

—Yours. To start.

—How is that? I haven't been wronged. I have nothing to forgive.

—It is still yours. I see that you hold my husband in contempt. As many people hold him in contempt, though he wronged none of them personally. Of course your forgiveness won't change those people's minds. Only one person's forgiveness can do that. But you are in a position to influence that person.

—There you are mistaken. Nobody is in a position to influence that person. Which is why he is that person.

—However he is, Svetlana said, her expression unbeguiled, he is a man.

At this Leora could not help but smirk.

—According to the latest news, Leora said, and she enjoyed the vexed, befuddled look on Svetlana's face.

—You don't have any idea what I'm talking about, Leora added.

Uncertain, cautious, fearful, Svetlana didn't answer.

—What happened between Baruch and me is all over the papers. Do you understand?

Before her, Svetlana leaned away, drew her teacup to her bosom, and straightened her spine to sit fully, rigidly upright, as though tensed against a cruel onslaught.

—So if you believe God sent us to you, you might want to question His timing. We have our own troubles. We came here to escape them. Only, as it turns out, we found new ones. In any case, Baruch's forgiveness will be of no benefit to your husband now. Right now, Baruch could use this sort of forgiveness himself. Not that he seeks it.

Rather than stiffen further, Svetlana appeared to relax. Her eyes lit with a sly, fervent, self-satisfied gleam.

—Then I wouldn't be so quick to question God or His timing. What you say gives me no reason to question Him. On the contrary, only to further admire His wisdom. Only He could contrive to bring us together at such a time. When we are all in such need. It is clear as day that everything is according to His will. I am surprised you don't see it. He brought you here not only for our sake but also for yours. You say that Baruch's forgiveness will be of no benefit to my husband, but how can you be so sure? If he is fulfilling God's plan, then it will be to everyone's benefit. And if it seems improbable, that is further proof that it is ordained. I see by your face that you still don't believe. You think I am a lunatic. But half the miracle has already happened. You are here. If half the miracle has already happened, it is lunacy to deny the other half.

Almost against her will, Leora's mind, as if of its own accord, step by step, advanced this hypothetical. Was there truly some advantage to be gained from this scenario?

Baruch Kotler, on the run with his young mistress, stumbles upon the man who betrayed him to the KGB. And forgives him!

And then what? A photo of the two of them clasping hands. Followed by the grand redemptive statement. But what was it? *This unexpected meeting has reminded me of my priorities: my family and my people. My commitment to my people has never wavered, but I have hurt my family and I will do whatever I can to make amends.*

This was the standard script. If she could distance herself from her feelings, she would advise Baruch to deliver these lines. As for if he would do it, that was another matter. In any case, what good would this confession do? Leora tried to continue thinking this way, pragmatically, minding Baruch's interests, but her pragmatic thoughts pragmatically branched off. Baruch's interests were one thing, but she had interests of her own. And if their interests diverged, what would happen to her? What place did the world reserve for the discarded mistresses of powerful men? When the unwelcome attention waned and people turned to the next disturbance, where did these women go? Were they allowed to slip into a quiet anonymity—marrying a gentle and understanding man, living in an unremarkable town, doing the grocery shopping with a child riding in the cart? But what if they wanted something more, to wield some of the power that had attracted them? How stubbornly did the world conspire against them?

—Look into your heart, Svetlana said. That's all I ask. You have the ability to save lives. And what does a person gain from withholding mercy?

At that moment the front door opened and there came the sound of Tankilevich's heavy steps. They both looked up to see him enter the kitchen, his face dark with disapproval at the sight of Leora.

TWELVE

Kotler stared for long minutes out the window and into the chicken yard. What had once seemed like the right decision, compulsory even, now seemed like utter foolishness. What had made him think that he could go on some romantic holiday when the situation at home was dire and his own son was caught up in it? He'd failed to understand his duty clearly. His duty was to see things through to their conclusion. When the army and the police came to evacuate the settlement, his duty was to be present, holding a placard: *Peace Settlement Before Settlement Withdrawal!* But he had convinced himself that he needed to leave. That the scandal would overshadow everything. That his presence would prove too distracting. That the helpful, reasonable thing to do was to absent himself. And he'd somehow thought that far away, in Crimea, he would be able to occupy his mind with other thoughts. Now, after speaking to Benzion, he saw his mistake. He had engaged in games. Coming to Yalta had been a game. And staying to confront Tankilevich, to satisfy his curiosity? Also a game. Well, he had played games for one day, and one day was enough. He'd caught a glimpse of Yalta and seen the changes fifty years had wrought. He'd had a day and a night together with Leora, the most he could ask for under the circumstances. If he was to have no more, he would have to accept it. That was the bargain he had struck on the park bench. And as for Tankilevich, what else did Kotler want? He'd seen as much as he needed to see. Enough, in any event, to resolve the central mystery. *Was Tankilevich living or dead?* Living. *How did he live?* Like this. *Had justice been served?* In its way.

It was still early in the morning. If they took a taxi to Simferopol, Kotler thought, they could be at the airport in two hours. If they were lucky, in another two hours they could be in Kiev. By the end of the day, they could be back home. Almost certainly too late for the evacuation, but not for the aftermath. The aftermath was also important—in its way, more important. The evacuation itself was by now a foregone conclusion. People could protest and resist, but the decision had been made and wouldn't be reversed. The aftermath, on the other hand, was an open question. And the aftermath accounted for the larger portion of life. The drab aftermath, when the vanquished must fend for themselves. He remembered it after Gaza—the dazed, disbelieving, resigned numbers sitting on the steps of their mobile homes. They had been deceived, misled. In a golden hour they had been promised one thing, and that promise had been rescinded. And what did they get in return? They got what Kotler had predicted. From the Arabs they got rockets—some people had apparently expected bouquets. Not that he blamed them for their optimism. They hadn't had his education. Even if a lesson was elementary, one rarely learned it in the abstract. The instruction had to be applied directly onto one's hide. Holding the territory had become increasingly painful, but as Kotler knew, one had to have a tolerance for pain. Because there is no life without pain. To deny this was only to invite more pain. This is what they had done when they withdrew from the Gaza settlements in 2005, and they were doing it again, as if a mistake stubbornly repeated could yield different results. To uproot thousands of your own people. To make casualties of them for no discernible purpose. It was gross incompetence. If you were not willing to protect your people, you should not have encouraged them to live in that place, and if you were not going to encourage them to live in that place, you should never have held the territory. There was no middle ground. Once you had committed to one, you had committed to all. The time for simply walking away had long passed. Now you stayed at any cost or exchanged a pound of flesh for a pound of flesh. That was all. Nothing else.

Well, what rigidity! Kotler observed with bemusement. Sometimes, after a run of such thoughts, he stood as if at his own shoulder, looking at a curious twin self. Who was the man who thought these thoughts? It came as something of a surprise. Not because of the thoughts—he didn't dispute the thoughts—but their pitch. The pitch of a public man who expected his thoughts to have injunctive force in the world. In spite of his true nature, he'd become this man. Forty years earlier, he'd been thrust, unwittingly, into this role by Tankilevich. Neither of them could have anticipated where it would lead. When he'd first seen the article in *Izvestia,* his head swam. Then, two weeks later, on the street outside his apartment, half a dozen agents swooped, surrounding him, their many hands clutching his coat and tossing him, limp as a rag, into the waiting car. From such pathetic beginnings he rose. Simply, he was forced to discover hidden reserves of strength. And once he rose, it was hard to return to the man he'd been before—a fairly ordinary man, with no grand designs. A former musical prodigy with small hands, a degree in computer engineering, and a desire to live in Israel. This described nearly every Zionist in Moscow. But then, after his ordeal, he was exposed to people in positions of power and saw how many of them were inadequate, even mentally and morally deficient. Little more than noise and plumage. And then it seemed impossible to leave serious matters—matters for which he had sacrificed everything—in the hands of such people. Still, he wasn't one of them and it was a wonder that he had lasted in their midst for as long as he had. Now, almost certainly, his time was up. How many politicians survived such a scandal? So why couldn't he now return to his original humble ambitions: to lead the life of an ordinary citizen in his ancestral homeland? How many other immigrants were there, even former refuseniks, who'd attained just that sort of life? They gloried in the country, found pleasure in every mundane detail. It all still seemed miraculous for a people so long displaced. Street signs bearing names from Jewish history. Hebrew singing issuing from the radio. The sight of young Jewish soldiers in uniform. All the peerless works of Jewish industry. Even the trees and birds, their beautiful essences nourished on Jewish soil. It sufficed for them. Only an egomaniac thought in terms any more exalted—to be a leader of the people, a second Moses or Ben-Gurion. But the question was, after he had been exposed to the upper machinations, to the sordid leveragings of power, and knowing what he knew, could it still suffice for him?

In the chicken yard, Tankilevich came into view. His legs

moved stiffly, arthritically, as if they had lost the greater part of their utility. He still had the presence of a large man, but he was sapped of strength, his arms depleted of muscle, the elbows bulbous in their sheath of skin. He carried weight in the stomach and chest, but it was slack and unwholesome. The only sign of vitality was his full, almost overfull, head of white hair, below which his face was drawn, his skin loose at the mouth and the throat. He gave the impression of dissatisfaction and ill health. Bent wincingly at the knees, he ducked his head and shoulders inside the chicken coop and then held this inelegant pose, his legs splayed for balance and the wide seat of his pants framed by the gray wood of the chicken coop. Kotler couldn't help but compare him to others from the movement, most of whom had passed through the frozen jaws of the Gulag to reach Israel. They'd emerged from captivity emaciated, jaundiced, and toothless, thinking that they would never fully recover. But to see them now, one would never guess. Kotler had recently visited Yehuda and Rachel Sobel at their home on the grounds of the Weizmann Institute. They had themselves a little villa. Pomegranate and citrus trees surrounded the backyard patio where they'd taken their dinner. Rachel had plucked herbs for their meal from ten different ceramic pots. Yehuda was tanned, stout, and percolating with good health. And yet the man had spent two years in a hole near the Mongolian border, much of that time with an abscess in his mouth. Or there was Eliezer Shvartz, who did his morning calisthenics on a balcony that overlooked the Jaffa Gate, and Abrasha Mirsky, who held several patents in desalinization and had retired to Ma'ale Adumim, and Moshe Gendelman, who had grown a long beard, fathered eight children, and ran a yeshiva in Kiryat Shmona.

Compared to Tankilevich, they were all thriving, each after his own fashion. From a certain standpoint, Kotler thought, Tankilevich had no right to look as terrible as he did. Nobody had tried to destroy his health. So it was disgraceful for him to be in such poor shape. Nobody had done it to him. He had done it to himself. Perversely, Kotler thought, though it served him right, he hadn't earned the right.

Tankilevich took two short shuffling steps back from the chicken coop and then extracted his shoulders and head from the enclosure. He straightened himself to his full height. In his hands he cradled several white eggs. Kotler couldn't tell how many. Perhaps half a dozen, perhaps fewer.

Eggs in hand, Tankilevich stood contemplative, gazing off to one side. Kotler remained at the window watching him. To watch another person think was absorbing, more absorbing than watching a person do anything else. Nothing was quite so personal or mysterious or telling. And all the more absorbing when it was someone you knew. To see him in an unguarded moment when he was trying to be known to himself. And more, to watch him when you believed he was thinking about you. Tankilevich peered down at his eggs and then again at a point over his left shoulder. Every fluctuation of thought had its corresponding expression, which could be read as though set in type: self-pity, reproach, accusation, defeat, forbearance.

Tankilevich turned his head and looked at the window behind which Kotler stood. There was no confusion. It wasn't nighttime, and the glass played no optical tricks. Kotler didn't flinch from Tankilevich's gaze, nor did Tankilevich avert his eyes. They looked at each other through the glass. And now what did he detect on Tankilevich's face? A flare of recalcitrance that quickly guttered. And what of his own face? What did Kotler present? The same expression he had presented to the KGB and all the subsequent adversaries. Unyielding calm. An expression of come-what-may. No—more than that. An expression that invited come-what-may.

Though it seemed to pain him body and soul, Tankilevich put one foot in front of the other and trudged toward Kotler. *If this is the way it is to be,* Kotler thought, *then this is the way it is to be.* He moved from the window and went to meet Tankilevich. If they were to have this encounter he preferred not to have it in this small room, contained and constricted, but outdoors, with the sun and the air and the expansiveness of the sky, as befit a free man.

THIRTEEN

Tankilevich stood in the yard, waiting for Kotler to appear. Along the wall of the house was a wooden bench—seven slats nailed together—and an upended zinc tub. Tankilevich thought to sit on the bench or to lay the eggs on the base of the tub. It had a lip that would keep them from rolling off. He bent and carefully placed the eggs down on the tub, his nerves and the need for concentration amplifying the geriatric tremor in his hands.

In the hallway, Kotler spied Leora and Svetlana in the kitchen. Both women eyed him expectantly. He acknowledged them with a quick cheery nod and continued to the side door. Stepping out into the yard, he saw Tankilevich stooped and intent over the metal tub, where the eggs rested in a line along the edge of the slightly convex surface. A hollow metal tapping sounded as Tankilevich put the last egg down with its fellows.

—I see you have your own little kibbutz.

—Oh yes, it's some kibbutz, Tankilevich said. We're four chickens from the grave.

—That's a lot of kibbutzes today.

—Too bad.

—I agree, Kotler said.

—How nice. Is that all? Or is there more you came to say?

Tankilevich had his first good look at Kotler in the flesh. Over the years, he had of course seen his picture in the papers and marked his progress. But to see a man in the flesh was a different matter. How had the years treated him? Forty years ago, he had been a skinny, quick-witted, balding, shabbily dressed young man. Shabbily dressed even for Russia in the 1970s. Tankilevich, who cared to dress better, had allowed himself to feel superior. Now Kotler was still shabbily dressed. His shirtsleeves were too long; the cuffs dangled. His trousers were baggy, even though he had gained weight. Only his shoes were worth envying. They were clearly from abroad, not something you could find at the bazaar. The shoes declared him a foreigner. The shoes and his expression. The easy, confident look of a person who lives his life in a better country. Kotler had prevailed and he had come to lord this over Tankilevich.

—Volodya—

—Chaim.

—Chaim, Chaim. For the last time, I didn't come here to say anything to you. I had no idea you lived here. Not in Ukraine. Not in Crimea. Not in Yalta. In fact, I had no idea whether you were living at all. Nor did I spend much time on this question.

—I wrote a letter.

—What's that?

—I wrote a letter. To Chava Margolis.

—And?

—Ten years ago.

—All right.

—She didn't tell you?

—Chaim, despite your fervent Zionism, it's clear you're not keeping up with the news from Israel.

—I keep up perfectly well. I watch the Russian television. I read the Russian press. And a friend informs me of the Hebrew. He gets it on the computer.

—Then perhaps this bit of news eluded you. Or perhaps it didn't rate over here.

—What news is that?

—The news of my Jerusalem trial. Chava Margolis was one of the witnesses for the prosecution. She and Sasha Portnoy. A few others too. The plaintiff was another activist. He made some outrageous claims against me in print. I defended myself and he brought a suit against me for libel. Shapira. From Gomel. Is the name familiar?

—No.

—Well, he had a very intricate thesis worked out, in which I had not been an agent of the American intelligence services, as you accused me of being, but rather an agent of the KGB. And that my Moscow show trial had been doubly fabricated. A show trial in which I, the defendant, had been in league with the authorities who were prosecuting me. In other words, I merely gave the very convincing impression of passionately defending myself and the Zionist movement, whereas, in fact, I was opposed to the movement and used the trial process as a way to expose other activists. Genuine activists like Chava and Sasha and, presumably, Shapira. And that it was because of me that they were imprisoned and exiled. You see? That I, who pretended to be the great hero, and who was celebrated above all the others, was in fact a traitor and a party to a deception of unprecedented complexity and mendacity. That I was heartless enough to put those closest to me, my parents and my young bride, through terrible anguish for more than a decade. And that while my family believed I was being kept in deplorable conditions in Soviet jails and camps, and while they moved heaven and earth to win my freedom, I was actually luxuriating in some undisclosed location, a client of the KGB. That, in essence, I was the worst traitor of all. Worse even than you.

—They mentioned me in the trial?

—Of course. You were my accomplice. Naturally. We plotted together.

One of the chickens had skittered over to them and now cocked its pert, imbecilic head at Tankilevich. With an angry swipe of his foot, he sent it flapping.

—When was this trial? he asked.

—Ten years ago.

—The same time I wrote to Chava.

—Evidently. Had I known you were alive, I could have called you as my witness.

—How so?

—To recount how we plotted together.

—No, we didn't plot together. But if, over my head, you plotted with the KGB, how would I have known about it?

—Over your head?

—Yes. It was in my letter to Chava. I explained everything to her. How I did not write that statement in *Izvestia*. How they merely appended my name.

—I see. And was it a look-alike who testified against me at the trial and confirmed the substance of the letter?

—It was I but under duress. They also had me on medication. It was all in the letter to Chava. Which I expected she would share with others.

—She might have shared it with others, but not with me. I haven't spoken to her since the Jerusalem trial. And I've seen her only once, unavoidably, at a gathering of refuseniks in the Ben Shemen Forest. What valuable information did she fail to impart to me?

—A great deal. But I can see that you're not interested in it.

—That's not true. But if by *not interested* you mean that I don't believe anything you say will change the material facts, that's right.

—The material facts?

—Facts that most sensible people—not conspiracy theorists—consider to be established. You gave false witness against me to the KGB.

—I gave, but I was forced.

—It was the Soviet Union; who wasn't forced? A few degenerates. But most people aren't degenerates. Everyone was forced. Some nevertheless managed to resist.

That second trial. Kotler avoided speaking or thinking about it. It had been a disgrace to them all. Even though he'd been acquitted, he'd come away wounded—in stark contrast to his Soviet trial, where, though convicted, he had come away invigorated. To sit in an Israeli courtroom and see Chava and Sasha looking at him with the same cold rectitude they had once reserved for the KGB. Terrible.

One afternoon in the courthouse cafeteria, he had seen Chava alone.

—*Why are you doing this thing, Chava?*

—*Because I looked objectively at the evidence, that's why. And it confirmed my suspicions.*

—*What suspicions were those?*

—*That you were always a self-seeker. Here as there.*

They had always been a fractious group. That wasn't news. There had been plenty of rifts and conflicts in Moscow. There were nearly as many deviations in their ranks as there had been among the Marxists at the time of the revolution. Not to mention the purely personal rivalries and antagonisms. But one had to expect some strife. Dissidents were by nature contrary. They would find fault with Paradise and send God a petition.

And how had they been to one another afterward, in Israel? Decent, for the most part. Ideological differences, irrelevant in Israel, were shelved. But there was even more. People who had buckled under KGB detention were pardoned. If they appeared at gatherings, they were not shunned. Outsiders were surprised by this. But if you had been through that life, you found it easier, not harder, to forgive. You remembered your own bouts of despair. Who among them was made of steel? Very few. Sobel had had it very hard. He'd held out remarkably. And Kotler would grant that both Chava Margolis and Sasha Portnoy were tough. He'd spoken with people in a position to know and had read their books. He didn't call their accounts into question as they did his. But others did the best they could. None of them was trained to undergo interrogations. At most, they had read Esenin-Volpin's "Memo for Those Who Expect to Be Interrogated." It counseled silence. But you could keep silent a week, two weeks, a month. Eventually you found yourself obliged to speak. Especially when the interrogator paraded facts before you, some of which were accurate. You knew that others were

talking and you asked yourself what you would gain by keeping silent. Why, by your principled silence, should you incur
the harshest sentence? Those were the rationalizations. Everyone entertained them. But this was the sad irony: Those who
had succumbed were forgiven, and he who had endured was attacked. Attacked precisely because he had endured and was then
celebrated for it. As if that too had been his doing. As if he'd
been in a position to promote his own cause. As if he hadn't
been locked up like all the others. So what explained his fame,
then? It certainly wasn't his good looks. If he had attracted a dis-
proportionate amount of the world's attention, it was because
of Miriam. Unlike Chava or Sasha or Shapira, he'd had a soul-
ful, determined, striking young wife who went from embassy to
embassy, from Hadassah to Hadassah, campaigning for his freedom. It wasn't his fault that the world liked a love story.

Now he had betrayed Miriam and there was another scandal.
How had he managed it? In one small life, to have so many scan-
dals. But it was as though the first scandal had predisposed him
to the others. If you have drawn the world's attention once, it is
easy to draw it twice. And easier still for some tawdry business.
If you give the world a love story, it is like a first installment.
Where the next installment is a hate story. Of which the world
will accept an infinite number. He had Tankilevich to thank for
his first scandal, his introduction to the world. He had Shapira's
spitefulness to thank for his second. For this one, he could
thank himself.

Kotler looked at the man before him. Tankilevich smoldered.
He who had every right to be angry wasn't, and he who had no
right was.

—Well, here we are, Chaim. However you believe we have

been brought together, we have been brought together. What shall we make of this brief encounter?

—What is there to make of it?

—I don't know. There was a time when I knew very well. In jail, especially in solitary confinement, I composed long speeches to you. Detailed, biting, and incontrovertible statements that would have reduced you to ash. If I'd preserved them all, they would have filled a library. I paced in my cell and recited them with the passion of Hamlet. What else did I have to do?

Kotler had composed speeches and letters and dialogues? Tankilevich thought. Well, he was not the only one. He thought he could have filled a library? Tankilevich didn't doubt he could have matched him volume for volume. But he wasn't going to bleat about it.

—I had a brother, Tankilevich said. What I did, I did only for his sake. To save his life. That is all. I had a younger brother who was a thief and a fool and I destroyed my life to save his.

—Destroyed *whose* life?

—Ah, Tankilevich said and brushed this off with a wave of his hand. You got thirteen years. All right, I am sorry for your thirteen years. But the way you were going, you must have expected it. And if they hadn't used me to hang those years on you, they would have used someone else. But I got the same thirteen years and however many more.

Tankilevich could practically see the years, heaped one atop the other in a moldering pile. His brother had been arrested in 1964. So it was now forty-nine years since he had handed over the reins of his life. He had just turned twenty-one. His brother was two years younger. With his parents, he went to the KGB office in Alma-Ata to beg for clemency. And in the end, his parents offered him on the altar to save his brother. His mother wept and his father demanded. Somehow he found himself with his brother's life in his hands.

—My brother smuggled eight molars' worth of gold and they sentenced him to death. He was reckless and arrogant, but he was only eighteen, hardly more than a child. What was I to do, let them shoot him?

—So instead of him, me?

—They were never going to shoot you.

—The charge was treason, a capital crime, which came with a daub of iodine and a bullet to the head.

—What daub of iodine?

—To guard against infection, Kotler said with a grin.

—Before you, Portnoy and Baskin were convicted of treason, and their sentences were commuted. The Soviets weren't killing dissidents anymore. It wasn't like under Stalin. Or under Khrushchev. Under Khrushchev they were killing people like my brother. Everyone knew it. They were shooting them or, worse, sending them to perish in the uranium mines.

—So what was the deal you made?

—I agreed to work for them. In exchange, they reduced my brother's sentence to ten years. He served eight and then went to bestride the world. While I sat in my Ukrainian village, he had Israel and America and Europe and even the New Russia. He traded, he did business, he had four wives, six children, and God knows what else. He lived like a king until some Moscow gangster put a bullet through his heart.

For that Tankilevich had forfeited his life. Though it would have been ludicrous to expect that his brother would recast himself as a scholar or a healer. His brother was a swindler, and Tankilevich had merely granted him the chance to live long enough to see the USSR remade in his image. In recompense, Tankilevich had received souvenirs and postcards, a few phone calls, fewer visits. But when they moved from the village to Yalta, when the KGB assistance dried up and he and Svetlana were reduced to living off their meager pensions, his brother had sent money. He hadn't stinted. What he sent was enough for them to buy the house and the car. And for as long as his brother lived, he had continued to send. A small fraction of his many millions, to be sure, but Tankilevich didn't fault him. Though when he was killed, the millions mysteriously evaporated. There wasn't even enough for Tankilevich to fly to Moscow and attend the funeral. Strangers buried his brother.

—You worked for them from 1964? How many others did you denounce? Kotler asked, and for the first time he felt a flash of the anger he had known in those years.

—Nobody else.

—All those years for me alone?

—That's all they ever asked of me.

—Did you know from the beginning that you would be required to denounce Jews?

—I didn't know anything. The colonel said I would have a chance to restore my family's honor by protecting the motherland from spies and saboteurs. I thought he had in mind catching others who were doing what my brother had done. Those who were doing it on a larger scale. But I heard almost nothing from them for several years. I guess they had no shortage of informants. They didn't contact me until 1972, when they made plans to move me to Moscow. Only then did they explain what they wanted from me.

—So you never applied to go to Israel.

—How could I? They had me by the neck.

—Well, you certainly played the Zionist.

—Before 1972, I knew as much about Israel as you did. I followed the Six-Day War. I watched the Munich Olympics. I never denied who I was. But what kind of Zionist could I have been in Alma-Ata before 1972? What did we have in Kazakhstan? I learned about Israel and Judaism along with you, in Moscow.

—As a KGB spy.

—It so happened I discovered Zionism through the KGB. But the things I learned, the people I met—those were the best days of my life. You say I pretended to care about Israel, but I cared as much as anyone else. I too dreamed of living there even though I knew that for me it was a futile dream.

—So if you were such a sympathizer, why did you continue to collaborate?

—In '72, they still held my brother. And after they released him, they threatened to take my father. He suffered from heart problems. I told them to arrest me instead, but they refused. They said if I stopped cooperating they would put my father under a rock and me right beside him. Even after your trial I tried to recant, but they wouldn't let me. I offered to go to prison, but they wouldn't allow it since it would compromise the result of your trial. I was the primary witness and so I couldn't be a criminal.

—We all had families, Kotler countered. We were all prey to the same intimidation. And we all had to make the same calculations. Everyone understood what it meant to shelter one's brother at the expense of someone else's. None of us had that right. You say you believed that they wouldn't shoot me, but how could you know? What if they *had* shot me? Or what if some accident had befallen me in jail that cost me my life or left me a cripple? Or even if none of this happened, what led you to think that I could be shorn of thirteen years of my life? That I should be separated from my wife? That my parents should not live to see me liberated? That they should have to meet death without their son at their side? There is no compensation for such losses. Not in this life. And no explanation but weakness. Which I can excuse. But not self-deception.

Kotler knew he was allowing himself to become overly emotional. It hadn't been his intent, but the mention of his father's death had loosed the stream of memories. Where had Tankilevich been when Kotler received the letter informing him of his father's death? What affront was he decrying while Kotler was at the Perm camp sewing hundreds of flour sacks? The letter arrived in February, four months after his mother had sent it. *My dearest son, How it pains me to give you this sad news.* The camp authorities would not explain why it had been so cruelly and illegally withheld. From there the conflict escalated so much that he himself came close to meeting his end. He announced a work strike. He would not sew the flour sacks. He wrote a protest to the post office, to the procurator's office, and to the Interior Ministry. Even though he was four months late, he decided to sit shivah. He stayed in the barracks and recited what mismatched scraps of Hebrew liturgy he could remember in the absence of a prayer book. *Hear, O Israel, the Lord is God, the Lord is One. Holy, holy, holy. He Who makes peace in the heights, may He make peace upon us, and upon all Israel, amen.* He wore the single phylactery upon his head like a horn, its companion missing, the subject of a previous battle. When he ignored the commands of the guards, the warden came to reason with him. He ignored him too. He was not deceived. After all, who had withheld his letter? Out of respect for his father, he declared that he would sit the full seven days and observe all the customs, neither working nor shaving. Then the battle started in earnest. They cut his food ration in half. But his bunkmates—a Crimean Tatar, a Jehovah's Witness, an Estonian nationalist—gave him from theirs. Before the week of mourning was up, the guards threw him into a punishment cell. When he still refused to concede, they confiscated his phylactery. Two guards pinned him to the stone floor while a third tore it from his head. He then had no choice but to declare a hunger strike until his property was restored to him. Ninety-eight days later, when his heart was no longer beating properly, the warden put the velvet pouch with the phylactery on the metal table beside his cot. For those three months, they had fed him with a tube down his throat.

But this was in the past and he had put it to rest. It didn't pay to dredge it up. Kotler looked at Tankilevich standing rigid before him.

—Never mind, Kotler said. It's all gone and done with.

—For who? Tankilevich asked.

—For everyone.

—Easy for you to say. You're a big personage. You have yourself a young mistress.

—You're right, I have a mistress. She's a remarkable young woman. Attractive, passionate, intelligent. Everything a man could want. But it's not a thing to gloat about. On the one hand, I am very happy with her; on the other, I regret the whole mess. I have hurt and embarrassed my children and my wife. I have damaged my reputation, but Shakespeare had a good line about that. Still, if you wish to insist on the past, then you can take credit for my mistress. If I hadn't been separated from my wife for thirteen years, it would never have happened. I would have gone to Israel shortly after Miriam. Maybe a year or two, but not thirteen. When we reunited, my Miriam would have been much as I remembered her. She would not have gravitated toward religion or the settlers. Neither of us was much inclined that way. We would have had a normal life. Instead, we had thirteen years of separation and thirteen years of struggle. She was alone fighting this battle. The state of Israel rebuffed her. Because I'd involved myself in the larger human rights movement, I wasn't Zionist enough for them. My case trailed unwanted complexities. So who embraced her and who helped her? The religious. The settlers. And naturally she was drawn into their midst. Because of their help, she had the strength to fight. For that I'm grateful. But the woman I found wasn't quite the woman I'd married. And as for Leora, my mistress, what reason would a girl like her have to be interested in a round little man like me? Only because I was dropped down the coal chute of the Gulag and came out the other end.

—There. That's it. Say what you will, but you benefited from this Gulag. You had thirteen dark years followed by how many bright ones? Without those thirteen years, where would you be? You say living a normal life. Am I living a normal life? Very well, in Israel a normal life doesn't look like this, but people still struggle. Maybe you would have had forty years like that? Instead you had money and position. Those thirteen years were your lottery ticket.

—I see. And you gave me this ticket.

—Look at it how you wish.

—All right. If I credit you with my mistress, I suppose I should credit you with the rest too. But what did it take to issue me this ticket? You did it, but anyone could have. With that legal process, anyone could have put his name to the indictment. And as you said, I was destined for trouble anyway.

—But it was I who signed. I explained to you why. And it is I who have borne the consequences all these years. To this day!

Tankilevich spoke the last with great vehemence, as though trying to breach the impenetrable divide between them. He had been too long maligned. It wasn't so simple as Kotler liked to believe. The force of his desire rose up in him like the sea. His head was filled with the deafening tidal rush. The white surf flooded his vision. His knees gave and he sank into it.

Kotler watched Tankilevich's eyes go blank, then quizzical. Tankilevich teetered and pitched to his side. Kotler was slow to react and reached for him only when it was too late. On the way down, Tankilevich's shoulder struck the tub, and with the blow the eggs juddered around the base. Three fell to the ground, surprisingly unbroken.

FOURTEEN

Kotler and Svetlana, each under one of his arms, helped Tankilevich into the house. He offered little assistance, shuffling his feet and mumbling unintelligibly. Leora followed behind.

They lugged Tankilevich through the kitchen and lowered him onto the sofa in the living room. His face was ashen. He continued to mumble. Now Kotler was able to distinguish a few phrases. *To strike a peaceful citizen, you scum! I have witnesses. I will report you to the police.*

Svetlana bent close to Tankilevich's face and pressed a hand to his forehead.

—Chaim, do you hear me? Chaim?

Leora entered from the kitchen, bearing a glass of water. She offered it to Svetlana, who accepted it without a word. She held it under Tankilevich's lips, urging him to drink. When he didn't respond, she set the glass on the magazine table nearby.

—We must call the ambulance, Svetlana declared.

There was a handset for a cordless phone on the table. Svetlana snatched it up and dialed.

—Has this happened before? Kotler asked.

Svetlana shook her head brusquely and, tight-lipped, held the phone to her ear.

Tankilevich had quieted. He was no longer mumbling but lying down with his eyes closed, breathing shallowly.

—Curse them, a person could wait all day, Svetlana seethed at the phone.

As she continued to wait for a response, Leora picked up the glass of water and moistened her fingers with it. She sat on the edge of the sofa and ran her fingers across Tankilevich's brow, temples, and the line of his jaw. She kept her fingers at his neck and felt for his pulse. All this she performed with precision and unexpected tenderness. In her care, Tankilevich began to breathe more regularly. Kotler watched and was gripped by a strong feeling of adoration. If this was how she cared for a stranger, an enemy, how indeed would she care for him? How could he contemplate losing such a woman?

—Is there a cloth or a handkerchief? Leora asked.

Svetlana, still loath to oblige, glanced around the room. She seemed on the verge of saying something to Leora when her call was connected.

—Yes, hello, Svetlana said, I need an ambulance.

As she spoke, Kotler dug into his pants pocket for his handkerchief and presented it to Leora. She doused it with water, and they both listened to Svetlana's conversation.

—It's for my husband, Svetlana said. He has lost consciousness.

Leora applied the compress to Tankilevich's brow and he

stirred a little. Reacting, it seemed to Kotler, either to the compress or his wife's agitated voice.

—He is seventy, Svetlana said. He suffers from arrhythmia, yes.

She listened, with growing consternation, to the voice on the other end and considered her husband.

—He is breathing, yes. No, I haven't taken his pulse or his blood pressure. When do you think I would have had time to do this? He is in distress. I am not a doctor. I called *you*.

His head cradled in Leora's lap, Tankilevich weakly blinked his eyes open. Kotler saw him inspect the room, looking first, dimly, at Leora and then, darkly, at Kotler and at his wife.

—I don't understand what you mean by busy, Svetlana said. You are the ambulance service. A person requires aid.

Tankilevich tried to lift his head to speak. His lips moved but his voice caught in his throat, producing no more than a croak.

—Maybe an hour, maybe two? What sort of answer is this? The devil take you!

She jabbed her thumb into the phone's keypad to disconnect and then glared at Kotler and Leora.

—This is the sort of country we live in! Where the average person counts for nothing. Less than nothing. You could drop in the street and nobody would bat an eye.

She bustled over to the sofa and edged Leora from her place. She cupped Tankilevich's head in her hands. He gazed at her with irritation. Again he tried to speak but his voice still failed him.

—Give him water, Leora said.

Petulant, resentful of another's instruction, Svetlana grabbed the water glass from the table and held it to her husband's lips. Tankilevich took a few feeble sips.

—No ambulance, he managed.

Svetlana studied him with overwrought concern. She felt his forehead with the back of her hand.

—Look at how pale you are. And cold.

Tankilevich stared at her silently, derisively, and then closed his eyes.

—I don't like the look of you, Svetlana said.

With this she turned and hurried out of the room and then noisily upended things in another. She returned carrying a blood pressure cuff.

—That one on the phone asks if I took his blood pressure. And what if I had? Would they come any quicker?

Tankilevich submitted as she fastened the cuff around his arm and inflated it with the rubber bulb.

—If you are old, they have no use for you. For a younger person, they might still come. But for an older person? Everyone knows. They don't come. Even if a person has a critical reading, they still don't care. An elderly person is having an infarction, better he should have it at home. If they send an ambulance, and he is still alive, they will have to take him to the hospital. And what then? He will occupy a bed. On an old person, they will be reluctant to operate. Why expend scarce resources? He might die on the table, or if he survives, what are the chances he'll last more than a week? Because this is a person with no money. If he had money, he would never have called the public ambulance. He would have called the private. And if he has no money it means he won't be able to afford the medications to recuperate properly. So, of course, why go to all the trouble to begin with?

Svetlana craned her neck to scrutinize the cuff's dial. She shook her head grimly.

—What does it say? Kotler asked.

—Eighty over fifty. Dangerous.

Svetlana removed the cuff from Tankilevich's arm and looked at her husband with a strange, rising fanaticism. She brought her face close to his and said in a loud, importunate voice, Chaim, can you hear me?

Tankilevich responded by squeezing his eyes shut and saying, almost soundlessly, Let me be.

—Let you be? Svetlana said, affronted. Not in your condition!

Tankilevich's response was silent disregard.

Svetlana continued to gaze at her husband as if to impress upon him her concern, but Tankilevich did not stir. He appeared to suffer both his wife and his debility. Svetlana persisted a moment longer before her expression changed, grew pensive.

—You can curse the system all you want, but what good is it? And what should we expect of the public services? The people who work these jobs are as bad off as everyone else. About the police, I already told you, Svetlana said, glancing at Leora. And this woman on the phone, what can her salary be? One hundred dollars a month? One hundred and twenty? How is she to live on it? The same for the paramedics. And if the hospitals don't have enough medicines and equipment, why would the ambulances? Consider yourself lucky if you get a blanket. If there was ever money to pay for such things, it was stolen long ago by the bureaucrats.

—You say there is a private service, Kotler said. If they will come, call them.

—And with what money? Svetlana inquired.

—If he needs help, call, Kotler said. I'll pay.

At this, Tankilevich stirred. He opened his eyes and tried, unsuccessfully, to lift his head. Failing, he looked acidly at Svetlana.

—I could call the Hesed, she said wanly. They have a service.

Tankilevich continued to glare Svetlana into submission.

She looked down at her husband miserably and wrung her hands.

—No. You cannot be left like this. I won't have it. It would be like I killed you myself.

But having spoken, Svetlana made no move. For some seconds, the only sound was Tankilevich's breathing. Then Leora plucked the phone from the table.

—What is the number? she asked.

—To what? Svetlana said.

—The private ambulance.

—I don't know it. I've never called.

—Find it, Leora said.

From the sofa came Tankilevich's strangled *No*. Leora ignored him and went with the phone into the kitchen. She returned holding the phone and some banknotes. She offered them back to Svetlana.

—This is the money Baruch gave you in advance for the week. You keep it. It's not charity. It's rightfully yours. If we choose to leave early, we're the ones breaking the agreement.

Svetlana vacillated, glancing at Tankilevich.

—Is it enough for the ambulance?

Svetlana nodded but still didn't reach for the money, as if she were in the grip of some paralysis. Leora pressed the bills into her hand.

—Find the number and I will call.

Svetlana looked down at Tankilevich, whose eyes burned in his pale face. She kneeled before him and took his hand.

—Have mercy on me, she said.

Tankilevich mutely shook his head.

Svetlana rose to her feet, gripped her hair by the roots, and startled Kotler with a piercing cry.

—There is nowhere to turn! Who can tolerate such a life?

Tankilevich closed his eyes and lay on the sofa impassively, deaf to the drama.

Svetlana directed herself at Kotler and Leora.

—Life here for us now is impossible!

Kotler looked at her and, incidentally, at the room, which was part of a house, on a patch of land, with a car parked in front, but he didn't contradict her.

—This country suffocates its people. Slowly, slowly, until it finally chokes you to death. That's where we are now. It's been suffocating us for years but somehow we managed to sneak a mouthful of air, but no longer. Now the time has come for us to choke, like everyone else who cannot leave this place.

—For Israel?

—For America. For Canada. For Australia. For Germany. Anywhere a mouse can find a hole. And, yes, for Israel. For Jews like my husband and half Jews like our daughters, and goy appendages like me. I understand very well how it is. We didn't treat the Jews fondly here. The Russians and the Ukrainians. We were terrible anti-Semites. With repressions and pogroms, our fathers and grandfathers drove the Jews from this country. Because we didn't want them here, the Jews had to make their own land. They shed their blood for it. A hundred years later and the Jews are nearly gone. So this is a great triumph! But how do we celebrate? By bending over backward to invent a Jewish grandfather so that *we* can follow the Jews to *Israel!* Ha! There is history's joke. But tell me who is laughing.

—Everybody and nobody, Kotler said. A Jewish joke.

—Nobody is laughing here. They are leaving or expiring.

—A sad end to the Crimean Jewish dream. And yet, if Stalin had only signed his name, it would have been a Jewish homeland.

—Yes, I heard of this dream. Stalin destroyed a lot of those people. But the Russians aren't the Germans and they don't pay reparations. So why speak of it? There is plenty of other history that also doesn't pay.

Tankilevich's chest rose and fell with a slow regularity. He lay on the sofa without stirring, reposed, as if calmly, pharaonically welcoming the void. Kotler recognized this condition, this state of being. A man proudly relinquishing his mortal coil. Where your death became your badge and a stab at your oppressors. This was how he had felt during the transcendent, soul-heightened stretches of his hunger strike. As though his hands were firmly gripped around the hilt of death, pointing its shining blade at iniquity. But what iniquity was Tankilevich combating? He would not accept Kotler's help on principle. For this he was willing to deprive himself of his life and bereave his wife and children. It seemed an act of pridefulness and spite.

—We should go, Kotler said.

He watched Tankilevich for a reaction, but the man offered none. Leora, who had resisted coming here from the first and had been agitating to leave, reacted hardly more. At this point, there was little in leaving to gladden the heart.

The only animated response came from Svetlana.

—That's it, then? she asked. This is how you'll leave us?

With that she cast her eyes at the dreary scene behind her. The room, even in the morning light, had a watery murk.

—I think we've done enough, Kotler said. We'll go before we inflict more harm.

—Never mind harm. The way we are, there's no more harm you can inflict on us.

—Your husband needs an ambulance. Because of me he won't accept one. We will go. And not just for your sake. We need to go. What Leora said is true. That money is rightfully yours. Use it to get him help.

Without saying another word, Kotler and Leora moved to leave the room.

—Go then, Svetlana cried. And turn your backs on God!

At this, despite his better judgment, Kotler failed to bite his tongue. A flicker of temper leaped in his chest.

—Excuse me, Kotler said, but let's leave God out of this for a moment. There is something I don't understand. You say you are to be suffocated and devoured. But how did you live, how did you feed yourselves all these years?

—How? We managed is how. We were younger, healthier. For as long as we could, we managed. We didn't ask anyone for a kopek. Even when we were eligible, Chaim didn't want to apply. He said, *I cannot go to them for money.* But we had no other choice. It was that or we become like the other pensioners in this country—insects scrabbling in the dirt. So I made him go to the Hesed. Not he, *I.* And how did the Hesed treat him? With compassion? With a shred of human decency? How? They humiliated a person. Here was a man who came to them in need, his heart full of love for the Jewish people, and they treated him like a dog.

Tankilevich lay, as before, with his eyes shut, but now he had shed the otherworldly affect. He was listening.

—Don't think to walk away with any rosy illusions, Svetlana spat. I understand, a respectable woman does not spill all her troubles. But I am not ashamed. Shame is a luxury, and we cannot afford it. My husband went to the Hesed as a Jew looking for help, and the director greeted him with a cold heart. She agreed to give, but imposed conditions. Conditions that my husband met for many years but that are now crippling for him. You see the state he's in. Who in good conscience would impose harsh conditions on a person like this? And now that he can no longer meet her conditions, she will revoke the subsidy. In other words, she's told us to dig our graves.

—What conditions? Kotler asked.

At this Svetlana hesitated and glanced at Tankilevich. He had opened his eyes and now looked at her scornfully, as at a simple-minded, bumbling child.

—He had to go once a week to Simferopol, Svetlana said tersely.

Kotler paused for a moment and smiled.

—The weekly trip to the synagogue, he said. To make the minyan.

In his pronunciation of the Hebrew word was a subtle mimicry of the way Svetlana had flourished it the previous day. She detected it.

—He would have gone willingly! Svetlana protested. When he was well, he went with pleasure. She'd only needed to ask.

But to force someone to perform a religious duty is an insult. An insult twice over. To the person and to God.

—I see, Kotler said. So this must be why God sent us to you.

—I don't presume to know God's reasoning. But just when our life here was made impossible, He sent the only person who could save us.

—I still don't understand how you believe I can save you.

—By letting us finally leave this place.

—For Israel.

—For Israel.

—Flights depart regularly from Kiev for Tel Aviv. I hope to catch one myself today. If your husband is well enough to travel, you could be on a plane tomorrow.

—Your girlfriend said the same thing. But both of you know it isn't so. We cannot go as we are. Not with my husband's past. He must first be absolved before the Jewish people.

—I see. And I'm to absolve him?

—Who else? Not me. If it were me, I would have done it long ago.

Tankilevich wouldn't accept Kotler's money—what of Kotler's absolution, to which he had an even fainter claim? Kotler looked to see if he was rousing himself in protest. He was not; instead, he had composed himself in a yet more stately guise, the image not merely of a man deserving of absolution, but of a man to whom it had been too long and cruelly denied. And thus—*tragically, tragically*—he might meet his Maker! It was clear that Kotler was expected to grant this absolution even though Tankilevich offered no repentance. But why should he? Since Tankilevich was in need, since he was in the subordinate position, he must be the injured party. And since Kotler was in the dominant position, since the power now rested in his hands, it was mean and petty of him to demand repentance, an admission of guilt. After all, guilt and innocence were not fixed marks. There were extenuating circumstances. Wasn't this the governing logic of the times? That cause and effect could not be easily disambiguated? That all was up for revision and nobody durst speak of an absolute truth? By this logic, in granting absolution, Kotler would be remediating a wrong. A wrong he had perpetuated by virtue of holding power. Saying *I forgive you,* he would actually be saying *Please forgive me.* Or, at least, *Please forgive me for not forgiving you sooner.*

There lay Tankilevich, presumably with one foot in the next world. Svetlana had asked Kotler to absolve her husband before the Jewish people. What would it cost him to say he would do it? A small lie. Just enough to calm her down and enable her to call the private ambulance. For Kotler wanted no hand in Tankilevich's death. Especially since, once, he had truly wished him dead. And yet, being himself, he still could not form the words.

—So, will you do it? Svetlana asked.

—Call the ambulance, Svetlana. First he needs to live, then worry about absolution.

From Tankilevich came another objection but it lacked force, and this time Svetlana did not heed him. She went into the kitchen and returned paging through a phone book. She looked from Kotler to Leora and then dialed the number. Unlike the call to the public ambulance, this one was brief.

—Shall we wait with you until they come? Kotler asked.

—What for? Svetlana said. So you can feel magnanimous? You gave the money for the ambulance. Very well. The paramedics will come. They will help us. Today. But what about tomorrow? If this is all you intend to do, then go, and the devil take you.

Now Svetlana went and sat again at her husband's side in a demonstration of fidelity. She placed a hand on his forehead, which caused Tankilevich to turn his face toward the back of the sofa.

The image of the two of them struck Kotler as pitiable and ludicrous. Upon these people he was to exercise his lofty principles? Still, Svetlana peered at him and awaited a reply.

—Svetlana, you may not believe it, but I harbor no ill will toward your husband. So it is not even a matter of forgiveness. I hold him blameless. I accept that he couldn't have acted differently any more than I could have acted differently. This is the primary insight I have gleaned from life: The moral component is no different from the physical component—a man's soul, a man's conscience, is like his height or the shape of his nose. We are all born with inherent propensities and limits. You can no more be reviled for your character than for your height. No more reviled than revered.

—You say, came Svetlana's answer. When you have been revered and my husband reviled.

—It's true. But that doesn't change the fact that it is so. You spoke before of fate, that you believe in a Divine Providence. You asked my opinion, and I said that I believed we walk hand in hand with fate. We choose to follow it or pull against it, depending on our characters. But it is character that decides, and the trouble is, we don't decide our characters. We are born as we are. Last night I told Leora about my father, who, in his youth, was a gifted sportsman, a very fast runner. I was his only child. In many respects I resemble him, yet I didn't inherit his athletic prowess. When I was a boy, he trained me, attempting to coax from me something that wasn't there. I tried with all my strength, but I simply lacked the ability. This was my first encounter with this unpleasant reality. The first but hardly the last. For instance, I was a good pianist. But if I didn't achieve greatness it was because, again, I lacked a certain quality that more gifted students possessed. I also had these small hands. I understood that both these things inhibited me equally and were equally beyond my control. It is the same with morality, as I was forced to discover. Just as there are people in this world who are imparted with physical or intellectual gifts, there are those who are imparted with moral gifts. People who are inherently moral. People who have a clear sense of justice and cannot, under any circumstances, subvert it.

—I see, so you were born a saint and my husband a villain?

—No, I do not consider your husband a villain. There *are* villains, but he is not one. This is why I said I don't blame him. He is an ordinary man who was ensnared in a villainous system. As for what I am, I don't have a word for it. A *saint* or a *hero* might be someone else's word, but not mine. I behaved the only way I could. When I was in prison and I knew that it would take only a single word from me to put an end to my suffering, I still could not bring myself to speak the word. It was like I had a plug in my throat. A moral plug. Impossible to dislodge. As for where it came from, that is as much a question for physicians as metaphysicians. This is what I discovered during my imprisonment. I saw the human character in its naked form. I saw at one end a narrow rank of villainy, and at the other a narrow rank of virtue. In the middle was everyone else. And I understood that the state of the world is the result of the struggle between these two extremes.

—A very strange idea you have, Svetlana said. There is no fault; there is no blame and no praise either. Nobody is accountable for his actions.

—I agree it is strange. There is no fault, no blame or praise, but we are all held accountable.

—I don't understand, Svetlana said. You say you do not fault my husband. You hold him blameless. You forgive him. But still you intend to punish him, even after all these years and him in his condition?

—I do not intend to punish him. But I cannot absolve him the way you ask. I cannot go in front of the news cameras and the journalists and declare to all the world that I forgive him and hold him blameless. That he was a victim of forces he could not resist. Even if this is what I sincerely feel in my heart.

—No? And why not?

—The reason I can't do it, the reason I'm forced to hold Volodya to account, no longer has anything to do with him. Even if I still believed that he deserved punishment for what he did, I agree that he has served his term, such as it is. If it were simply between him and me, I would say it: Volodya, I forgive you. But I can't go before the world and say that he was not culpable for his actions. Because the world would misunderstand.

A groan emanated from Tankilevich, and, as if with his last strength, he gripped the sofa and tried to lift himself up. Svetlana's hands fluttered about him, as though trying to dissuade and assist him at once. And he responded in kind, repelling and requiring her until he achieved a sitting position. He propped himself, somewhat precariously, against the arm of the sofa. But he was burning to speak.

—It's all very clear, Tankilevich said. You are the Shield of David protecting Israel from my toxic influence.

—That isn't what I am saying, Volodya.

—What you are saying is that I was not born a man but some sort of worm. And that most men who roam the earth are also worms. But as one such worm, I can tell you that if I had it to do over again, I would choose just as I did. If I hadn't agreed to work for the KGB, they would have killed my brother. And for all the trouble I caused you, you survived and prospered. So now you tell me how you, a man, would have acted differently.

Kotler looked unwaveringly at Tankilevich.

—Haven't I already answered that question? Kotler said. I couldn't have done what you did. Sooner than betray any of my brothers, I was prepared to die, to lose my wife, and to abandon my parents to a lonesome old age.

Kotler looked to Leora, who had observed all this coolly and silently. It was a coolness extended even to himself, he felt. As if he'd been weighed in the balance and found wanting. He'd never sensed it from her before.

He turned back to Tankilevich and addressed him as gently as he could.

—Here is what I will say to you, Volodya. And I say it without malice. Israel doesn't need you. It has thousands like you. Thousands of old generals on park benches plotting the next war with the Arabs. It can do without another. So why go to a place where you are not needed? Why not ask instead: Where am I needed? Where do my people need me? And choose that place. Choose that place, for the first time in your life, of your own free will.

—Choose to wither away, the last Jew in Crimea.

—If so, a noble end.

—If it's so noble, then why me and not you?

—Because I am still needed elsewhere, Volodya. Though I'm not sure for how much longer. I may yet join you here. We can both be the last Jews of Crimea or, God knows, part of another exile, another return.

Kotler checked his watch and looked out the window. There was no sign of the ambulance.

—We should pack, Kotler said. We should go.

He took a step in the direction of their room and glanced at Leora to see if she would follow. She did, though her face retained the same cool, inscrutable cast.

Kotler had taken several more steps when he recalled one last thing. He turned back to see Tankilevich now lying on his back again, his eyes open as Svetlana peered anxiously at him.

—Volodya, Kotler spoke.

Tankilevich inclined his head toward him.

—The night before your letter appeared in *Izvestia,* you broke all those plates in our apartment. Do you remember?

He waited for Tankilevich to respond, to evince the least animate gesture.

—Do you remember? Kotler repeated.

—I remember everything, Tankilevich said slowly.

—I never understood it. What happened there? All those broken plates. And then sitting in the kitchen to glue them together.

—What happened? Tankilevich said. Very simple. I needed to do something with my hands. It was either that or I kill you. And spare us both.

Ascent

FIFTEEN

Once more, as on the previous day, Kotler and Leora, trailing suitcases, made their way among the sunburned vacationers on the esplanade. It was still before nine, but the day's procession had already begun. Was there another people who approached the phenomenon of leisure as systematically as the Russians? Was there a people who took the sun and the waters with more conviction and diligence? Natural remedies, holistic treatments, folk cures, mineral therapies—and the doctors and professors and experts who promoted them. The rival flows of mysticism and science that irrigated the Russian heart, a manifestation of the failed Soviet project. Backwardness yoked to forwardness. This was one of its more harmless manifestations. His father had embraced it. At dawn, he would already be walking along the shore, vigorously swinging and rotating his arms. By seven, he would have claimed a strategic spot on the beach. Soon after, Kotler and his mother would join him. Throughout the day they would follow a salubrious regimen of walks and swims because it was not acceptable to simply laze about. The sunlight contained vitamins. Walking at a prescribed pace improved the circulation. Immersion in salt water restored the skin. And the quality of the air for the respiratory system! And the aromatic wildflowers for teas and infusions! And the pleasure his father derived from the word *nutrient!*

Kotler and Leora picked their way through the vacationers toward the Internet café. Like the last Jewish stragglers, Kotler thought, with their suitcases and cheerless expressions in the holiday sunlight. Though, technically, that sad distinction belonged to Tankilevich. Capricious fate had cast him as the final link in the long chain of Crimean Jewry. A chain that stretched back more than a thousand years to the Khazars, the last Jewish warriors and emperors, if legend was to be believed. The Khazars, the Krymchaks, the Karaites. And, in the past century, the doomed farming colonists and Yiddish poets who had imagined a homeland in Crimea, a New Jerusalem to supplant the Old. Now it was coming to a close, like all Jewish stories came to a close, with suitcases.

There were only two other people in the Internet café when they arrived. Two young women typing quietly at opposite ends of the room. Between them were half a dozen vacant machines. The raucous boys waging war were gone. It was too early for them. Or perhaps the dark room with the strobing screens could not compete with the offerings of a summer morning. This could be construed as proof that the world was not yet beyond repair.

As before, Kotler and Leora took two neighboring machines. They propped their suitcases behind their chairs and started to seek their way home. In no time, they had it. At midnight, a flight departed Kiev for Tel Aviv. At eight in the evening, a flight departed Simferopol for Kiev. Seats were available on both flights. They could purchase them in a matter of minutes through the computer. Kotler reached for his wallet and his credit card. Leora stopped him.

—It is the same airline, Leora said. I will call to see what they charge to change the tickets.

—Unfailingly prudent, Baruch said.

—I see no reason for you to throw any more of your money away.

—Any more? Do you mean what I gave to Tankilevich?

—I mean this entire trip, Baruch. It was a mistake.

She spoke the words with a cold stoicism, the lingering effect, it seemed, of whatever had disturbed her at Tankilevich's house.

—The fault is mine, Kotler said. Forgive me.

—You don't need to apologize. Nor do you need to absolve me before the whole of the Jewish people.

Leora reached into her purse, took out her phone, and dialed the number for the airline. Kotler watched her as she waited for the system to connect and then as she submitted to the gauntlet of recorded prompts. Sensing her mood, he left her to the task and turned to his computer screen to key in the address for *Haaretz*. Unlike the previous day, he was not greeted by an unflattering image of his own face. His story had already dropped several rungs down the news ladder. Besides, his story had only ever been preliminary to the main story. And that story, after its interminable lead-up, was now in the offing. On the screen appeared the opening stages of the drama: Stricken, grieving, furious settlers facing columns of distressed and stone-faced Israeli soldiers and police. A young Orthodox mother, hardly older than a girl, in head scarf and long skirt, thrusting her squalling infant into the face of a young female soldier. A group of young men, with the long, flowing *payos* and the disheveled dress of the hilltop youth, who had chained themselves to the ark in a synagogue. A different group of men, older, who had each donned the striped costume of the concentration camp inmate, with the crude yellow Star of David sewn over the breast. The full shameful, histrionic, heartrending pageant was on display. He motioned for Leora to look. She gave a cursory glance, no more.

Kotler entered the address of *Yedioth Ahronoth* and found essentially the same images. He scanned the photographs for Benzion's face. In their uniforms and helmets, a number of boys resembled Benzion, more scholars than warriors, but none was Benzion himself.

Kotler felt a redoubled urgency to get home, if only, during such a turbulent moment, to breathe the same air as his countrymen. It was disgraceful to be away.

—Is there anyone there to speak with? Kotler asked Leora.

She nodded her head but said nothing. She was no longer pressing buttons, simply listening and waiting.

—I'd sooner pay the money than wait. To have the tickets would put my mind at rest.

—Another minute, Leora said. If they don't answer.

Kotler could see it was now a matter of principle. There was life: a quick leap from practical to principle. But he did not press her on it. If it had become a matter of principle, grounds for her to assert herself, it was because of him. She'd conceded one thing after another on this trip.

—Very well, Leoraleh, another minute, he said.

He used his minute to navigate from the news site to his

e-mail account. He'd last consulted it in Kiev more than a day ago. Then, there had been a block of messages forwarded from his office. Media requests. Now he saw more of the same. As well as a few notes from disparate friends, expressing, he assumed, some manner of concern or support or, perhaps, censure. He didn't open them. He scrolled quickly through the list, looking for anything that might require his immediate attention. His eye stopped on a message whose sender was identified as Amnon. Its subject line was a single Hebrew word: *Chaval*— "Too bad." Kotler clicked on it. The message contained no other text, only a picture of himself sitting on the park bench behind the Israel Museum. In his lap lay the sealed envelope with the photographs. Behind him rose the carob tree and the plum-colored, twilit sky. But beside him, where Amnon had been sitting, the bench was vacant. Any trace of Amnon had been meticulously erased, as though he had never been there. The only indication that there was something amiss about the photo was that a little lark had been placed atop Kotler's bald head. The bird perched there, making him look ridiculous. Like some dotty old fool or comic Saint Francis.

Kotler deleted the message.

He continued to scroll through the list and saw, one followed by the other, a message from Benzion and one from Miriam. Benzion's had been sent a little more than an hour before. And Miriam's only a few short minutes ago. Which meant that she would have pressed the button to speed it through the circuitry while Kotler was sitting in the Internet café. Thus he could envision her in their apartment, facing the computer screen, in the room they had designated as the office, the window at her back with a view of Mount Scopus, and on the wall above the computer screen the framed black-and-white portraits of his parents and her parents, taken around the same time though thousands of Soviet kilometers apart, both couples young and unsmiling, humbly dressed, embarking on new lives in the jagged aftermath of the war, daring to look with their dark eyes to the future. How would he fare under their scrutiny and judgments if they were here today? No, that was too simplistic, too self-critical. After all, their parents, like most people, had seen and sampled life's full panoply. So, the truer question was, how would he and Miriam both fare under their scrutiny and judgments?

The subject line of Miriam's message was blank. Benzion's read: *Psalm 137:5.* Kotler opened it first and discovered that the message consisted solely of the subject line. As if Benzion had composed it either very hastily or very cryptically. Kotler knew the Psalms reasonably well. He'd had occasion to read them in Moscow in his refusenik days, and in prison camp—from the Russian Bible kept by the Jehovah's Witness—he'd read them even more closely. With their calls for God's strength and protection in the face of wicked and ruthless foes, they'd seemed especially pertinent. He found in the Psalms, if not quite religious conviction, then something more vital to him, a sense of continuity with his people from deepest antiquity, with King David himself, who was made palpable through his verse as a man of flesh and blood racked by the same fears as Kotler was. *They encourage one another in an evil matter; They converse of laying snares secretly; They ask, who would see them?* And from King David he felt linked to the cumulous generations of his forebears, bowed under the harsh decree, who had also sought comfort in these words. From this history of Jewish resistance he had drawn his strength. The title of his memoir, *Song of*

Ascent, Kotler had taken from the Psalms, and its epigraph from Psalm 126: *They that sow in tears shall reap in joy.*

Off the top of his head, Kotler could not recall Psalm 137, and certainly not its fifth verse, but it was a problem that was easily solved. It no longer required a Bible. He typed the query into the computer and was met by the well-known opening:

> *By the rivers of Babylon,*
> *There we sat down, yea,*
> *We wept,*
> *When we remembered Zion.*

Its fifth verse read:

> *If I forget thee, O Jerusalem,*
> *Let my right hand forget her cunning.*

So he had Benzion's answer. The son had gone against the wishes of the father. It was nothing new. It accounted for the greater part of human history. Still, it didn't make it less of a mistake in Kotler's eyes, only a mistake for which he shared the blame. After the disgrace the father had visited upon the family, could the son have chosen differently? After such a thing, could he have been expected to quell his conscience and abide by his father? Even without the scandal, Kotler did not know what Benzion might have done. He actively believed in the things Kotler regarded as only ornamental, contextual. For Benzion, the God of Israel was the giver of the law. For Kotler, God and His law merely provided the inflection for the Jewish people. To be a Jew, one did not need to worship, only to be suitably inflected. To resonate at the Jewish semitone. Kotler knew many such people. Not only godless but God-averse. It was such people, after all, who had founded the country. It was from them that Kotler had drawn inspiration when he was his son's age, a dissident in Moscow. Weizmann, Ben-Gurion, Jabotinsky, Trumpeldor. For them the Bible was more a source of poetry and ancestral lore and less a guidebook for keeping house. But their example was waning. For Miriam and Benzion, the poetry and the lore were inextricable from the housekeeping. It was divine, which meant all or nothing. It was holy scripture, not a document to prove hereditary land claims. Which was very well. This line of thinking had always existed and there was space for it. But, increasingly, it left less and less space for anything else. Less space, as loath as Kotler was to admit it, for him and those like him. But wasn't that the dissident's lot? He should have been inured to it by now. Too much logic and so always the misfit.

Kotler looked to Leora, who was still holding her phone to her ear in silence.

—Benzion refused orders, he said.

Leora turned her face away from the phone.

—How do you know? The news?

—I don't know if it has made the news yet. He sent me a message. A verse from the Psalms. Its implication seems clear enough. We should order the tickets.

Leora nodded reluctantly, prepared to concede, but then a voice sounded through the handset.

—Hello, yes, hello, Leora said.

She was drawn into the conversation, which left Kotler to return to the computer screen and Miriam's waiting message.

He saw her name, *Miriam Kotler*, composed in Hebrew letters, as though she were asserting in the most unmitigated sense—before God and man—her connection to him. In those two words—her name—was enfolded their entire history together, a history of nearly four decades. From the time they had met in Moscow as fledgling Zionists, as Boris Kotler and Milena Ravikovich, to her becoming Milena Kotler on their wedding day. It was *Milena Kotler*, in Russian, that she had written on the first envelopes she mailed to him from Israel. Later, after his detention and the start of her campaign on his behalf, she became Miriam. For the duration of his sentence, that was the name he saw, again in Russian, on the post he was fitfully granted. Only after his release did he encounter this Hebrew version, spelled out on the directory of the apartment building where she had insisted on listing them both, *Baruch and Miriam Kotler*, years before there had been any tangible hope of a reunion.

Ah! It was wholly unpredictable where life's emotional jolts would come from, thought Kotler. He would never have supposed that the sight of Miriam's name, typed in Hebrew—a thing he had seen a thousand times on the ephemera of household bills—could so stir him.

He clicked on her message.

My Dear Baruch,

I don't know where my letter will find you, but I believe it will find you. This is the opposite of how it was all those years ago when I knew where you were but couldn't trust that my letters would be delivered. Much has changed since then, most of it, praise G-d, for the better. I have been reminding myself of this during these last two trying days.

Baruch, I never thought the time would come when I would be writing you such a letter. I never thought there would come a time when I would not know where to find you in this world. That has been the greatest shock of all. That, if you can believe it, is what seems most painful to me. That you have vanished on us. On me and on the children. That you have treated those dearest to you like informers, like strangers. Somehow I feel that if I knew where you were, I could better withstand my pain.

Baruch, I am not naïve. I understand that the promises people make to each other when they are young cannot be enforced when they grow old. I understand about men and the temptations of the flesh. I understand it from life and from our Torah, which does not shy away from this subject. I am a sixty-year-old woman and I know that, as pertains to the sexual appetite, this is not the same as being a sixty-year-old man. I do not desire and do not need to be desired the way I did when I was a younger woman. G-d, in His wisdom, made men and women differently, and made men to harbor these desires until their dying days. When King David was old, it was a young girl, Abishag the Shunammite, who was sent to warm his bed and not Bathsheba, his wife, whose beauty had once caused him to commit a terrible sin. The Torah never says how Bathsheba felt about this girl in her husband's bed. Did she not wish to care for him herself? Or did she accept that she could not provide for him the way a young girl could? Of course, those were different times and a king had many wives and none could make an exclusive claim on him. Still, I have been thinking about Bathsheba and Abishag these past days. There is only one passage in the

Bible where Bathsheba and Abishag appear together. It is when Bathsheba goes to King David to ask him to honor his promise to her and to appoint Solomon the rightful heir to the throne of Israel. "And Bathsheba went in unto the king in the chamber.—Now the king was very old; and Abishag the Shunammite ministered unto the king.—And Bathsheba bowed, and prostrated herself unto the king." Why does the Bible mention again that Abishag was with the king? It must be only to further humble Bathsheba at this moment. Not only must she beg her husband to keep his promise, she must do it before the young woman who now warms his bed. But in the end, she is rewarded. Her husband keeps his promise and her son ascends to the throne and builds the first temple, praise G-d.

I have been thinking about this and about what lesson I am to draw from it. Is it to accept that there is something in the natures of men and women that must be accommodated? I know that our intimate life is no longer what it was. I am not Abishag. I am Bathsheba. I am your wife, a woman of sixty, the mother of your children. But after all these years of marriage, what can Bathsheba ask of her husband? Can she ask only on behalf of the children, or also on her own behalf? If I no longer possess all the same desires, it does not mean I am without desires. I still desire those other things that we have always had together—comfort, familiarity, respect, affection, and love. For all the years we have spent together and the hardships we have endured, what is the value of the bond between us? What is owed to Bathsheba?

I am not writing to plead with you or make demands. I also will not pretend that you have not hurt me or that I am not angry with you. But I see that our life together has reached a crossroads and I ask myself which path I would prefer we take. It is true, we have both reached a very mature age and our children are nearly grown. We are no longer in that stage of life where we must worry about remaining together for the sake of the children. And I am past the stage of my life where I would be lost without a man. My mother was widowed when she was not much older than I am now and she lived until the end by herself. She claimed she was content. She would have preferred to have my father beside her, but without him she had the company of her friends and she also had me. Not only me, but all of us, as you well remember. We all cared for her, you no less than me. You were as much a son to her as if you were hers by blood. I too have friends and I have our children. And in time—soon, if G-d grants—there will be grandchildren. I imagine myself living the life my mother lived in her final years and I cannot say it terrifies me. But just as my mother would have wished to have my father by her side, I would still, even after all this, prefer to have you by my side. We have built this family together. It was the dream we shared almost from the first moment we met in Moscow. It seemed such a distant dream, and for so long it seemed nearly unattainable. But we have done it. We have made our lives in the land of Israel, the land of our forefathers, and we have raised two beautiful children here, proud Jews and Israelis who now dream their dreams in Hebrew.

Baruch, I don't know what your intentions are. I don't know what is in your mind or in your heart. I don't know what promises you have made to Leora, the Abishag in our story. Of course, I always recognized her as Abishag. A younger woman in your house is always Abishag. No matter how doting or polite she may be, you know she poses a threat. It is not even her fault. It is in nature. Our part is to struggle against nature. Our part is to resist our bad inclinations with our good. I do not know how much Leora resisted her bad inclinations and I don't know how much you resisted yours. But Dafna said you were blackmailed and that, if you had compromised, those dreadful photographs would have been suppressed. (On this, I took your side. One cannot make such compromises and I know you never would.) But if you were blackmailed it means that you did not intend for those photographs to be seen and you didn't want to make public this affair. And perhaps this affair had already run its course or you were planning on ending it. Perhaps it was never your intention to leave our marriage. Perhaps you had simply strayed, submitted to an isolated temptation, and were now prepared to continue with our life as we have always lived it. That is for you to say. But if you wish to return to our marriage, I am willing to forgive. Our friends, our community, the people who have rallied around me as they rallied around me in the years of our earlier struggle, feel as I do. Everyone is willing to forgive. No one of us is perfect. Just this morning, Gedalia brought me this verse from Ecclesiastes: "For there is not a righteous man upon earth, that doeth good, and sinneth not." Our greatest sages and prophets were also not without sin. So what right do I have to expect of you, even you, to be more righteous than our sages?

Baruch, whatever you decide, I ask only that you don't delay. Even if you decide not to return to me, return speedily to

*the country and to your children. They are in desperate need
of your presence and your guidance.*

Your wife,
Miriam

How thoroughly he had fouled the best of what they had once
been, Kotler thought. And of the many offenses he had committed, the worst seemed to be against the girl he had met in
Moscow forty years earlier to whom he had pledged his love. The
quiet, contemplative beauty, like a young Ingrid Bergman, who
appeared one evening at the Hebrew class that the Sobels ran secretly out of their apartment. *Rak Ivrit*—"only Hebrew"—was
the rule. In the course of a conversational exercise, he had said to
her: *Would you like to see a movie and go drink coffee and get married and move to Israel and raise a large family?* To which she had
replied with the single Hebrew word: *Zehu?* "That's it?"

Somewhere within Miriam this girl was cradled, and also
the other Miriams who, through selflessness and loyalty, had
enriched and solaced his life. He had wronged them individ-
ually and collectively, but they were now out of reach and he
could not return to them even if he wished. And to the Miriam
who had written the letter? Likely he could not return to her
either.

Leora's telephone conversation had ended before Kotler finished reading Miriam's letter. Perceptive to the last, she didn't
disturb him but waited patiently for him to conclude.

—Something important? she asked.

—A letter from Miriam.

—Anything I should know?

—Nothing new, Kotler said as kindly as the words could be spoken. Other than some wisdom from Gedalia.

—And what is that?

—"For there is not a righteous man upon earth, that doeth good, and sinneth not."

—He would know.

They did not pursue it further. They were of the same mind about Gedalia, though Kotler had reasons beyond those Leora could know. It was a young Gedalia, barely out of yeshiva, who had been Miriam's chief advocate and protector. Her chaperone on her global crusade to free Kotler. There had been salacious murmurings, which had reached Kotler even in prison. In her letters, Miriam denied them, but not long after Kotler landed in Israel, Gedalia came to him, beating his breast, begging forgiveness, tearfully confessing to his impure thoughts and desires.

—I got our tickets changed, Leora said.

—Yes, I overheard. Thank you.

—No need to thank me, Baruch. It felt good to finally manage something. Even something so trivial.

Kotler looked at his watch. Half past nine. They had more than ten hours before their flight to Kiev. If they left now, they would be facing an inordinate wait at the Simferopol airport. It would be an inordinate wait in any airport, let alone Simferopol, which was not among the world's coziest way stations.

—I suggest we go to Simferopol, Leora said. At the airport or the bus station we could stow our luggage and see the city. There must be something to see there.

—There must, Kotler said.

—What else would you propose? Leora asked.

—We'll be the only tourists to leave Yalta without seeing the Livadia Palace, Chekhov's house, or Massandra Beach.

—So you have a reason to come back, Leora said.

—No, Leoraleh, Kotler said. I have no reason to come back.

To reach the taxi stand they crossed Lenin Square for the last time. An accordionist, older than Kotler, a roostery fellow in a white baseball cap, had set himself up at the base of the statue. On the ground, lashed to a wheeled dolly, a stereo system piped an underscore of music. Next to the stereo sat an accordion case, open to receive contributions, a few bills and coins already scattered on its incompatibly lush blue velvet lining. The accordionist stood by the case and fingered the melody of a Russian folk song. A small audience formed a perimeter to listen to the music and watch the bolder among them dance. Kotler also slowed to watch, and Leora fell austerely in line beside him. On the impromptu dance floor, some dozen people spun. Kotler counted only one man among them, a youth with a shaved head who led his slim girlfriend by the hand. The rest of the dancers were older women. Some danced in pairs a short distance apart, stepping to the music. The others danced by themselves. They looked like ordinary embattled Russian women of Svetlana's type briefly forgetting their arduous lives. Nearest to Kotler danced a woman in a flowered blouse and a long white skirt, her figure matronly, her hair auburn but gray at the roots, the skin of her face finely wrinkled. She held her head upturned, her shoulders level, her hands delicately twirling. She revolved in a small circle, her feet moving under the sweep of her skirt. On her feet, Kotler saw, she wore flesh-colored nylon socks and white leather, low-heeled shoes. With a blade she had cut the leather to make room for her bunions, which bulged almost monstrously through the rents.

Everywhere you look, heartbreak, Kotler thought.

At the taxi stand, cars were waiting. Kotler approached the first. Its driver sat inside, his window rolled down, reading a newspaper on the steering wheel.

—Will you take us to Simferopol? Kotler asked.

—And why not? the man replied. I'd take you to Kherson. The farther the better.

He named a fee and took charge of their bags while Kotler and Leora deposited themselves in the backseat, Leora turning to face the window, withdrawn into herself.

They drove along the same road they had taken before, this time heading out of Yalta. Morning traffic was heavy through the tourist center. Cars and buses lurched forward. Kotler gazed out the window at the view of sparkling, modernized Yalta. A resort town in a corrupt country, as it had always been, there to propagate the illusion. But he had loved it as a boy and believed his parents had loved it too. Now he would leave it for the last time and consign more of his life to the impervious past.

They picked up the main highway and drove through the Crimean countryside. They saw again the scenery they'd seen through the bus windows the previous day: the small towns and villages, visible from the road, little changed from fifty years earlier. They were ramshackle then; they were ramshackle still— though topped, here and there, by a satellite dish. Twice on the way to Yalta their bus had stopped to allow a herd of goats to cross the highway, their minder blithely leading them as though privileged by the antiquity of his trade. Sometimes they saw workers in the fields; sometimes men in the bones of a house engaged in some ongoing construction project. The pace of everything seemed governed by a bucolic torpor. It resembled,

Kotler thought, Israel not so very long ago and, even to this day, the Arab parts of the country in the north and the south. The main difference was a peculiarity of the landscape, crude structures strewn haphazardly everywhere. Often they were just four walls without a roof. Or if with a roof, then with gaping holes for the windows and doors. All were of the same yellow limestone and could just as easily have been new and unfinished as old and decaying. But if they were old, Kotler didn't remember them from before. The previous day, on the bus to Yalta, he'd turned to a young Russian man in the neighboring seat. Drily, the man informed him that these were the instruments of a Tatar land grab. After the fall of the Soviet Union, the Tatars had returned to Crimea in their thousands. The Ukrainian government, bowing to their historical grievances, had ceded them land wherever they built dwellings. These were supposed to be their dwellings.

Land! The land! What, Kotler had wondered, would his old Tatar prison mate have made of this? The repatriation and autonomy of the Crimean Tatars had been his struggle. He had given his life over to it. Were he still living, he and Kotler could have had an interesting conversation. What dreams they had nurtured and what distortions now obtained. And it was all to do with land. A measure of earth under your feet that you could call your own. Was there a more primitive concept? But nobody lives in the ether. Man is a physical being who requires physical space. And his nature is a prejudicial nature of alike and unalike. That was the history of the world. How much earth can you claim with another's consent? How long can you hold it if you haven't consent? And is it possible to foster consent where none exists? Kotler didn't know the answers to the first two questions, but the essential question was the last, and the answer to that was not favorable.

—Imagine, Kotler said to Leora, this could have been the Jewish homeland. Then the Tatars and the Russians could have demanded we go back to where we belong, as the Palestinians do now.

Leora sat on her side of the backseat as she had from the start, looking silently out her window. Kotler had spoken in an attempt to break the silence, make a conciliatory gesture, though he still didn't know exactly what he'd said or done to alienate her.

—If you have something to say, Leora, you should say it. Mindful of the driver, Kotler spoke the words in Hebrew. We have two hours in this car.

Peevishly, Leora turned from her window.

—What are you doing with me, Baruch?

—I don't understand.

—Why did you get involved with me?

—I thought that much was clear. I fell in love with you.

—So you said. But how could someone like you fall in love with someone like me?

—Someone like me? Someone like you?

—An exceptionally moral person like you and an ordinary person like me. I don't understand how that is possible.

—It is possible. It happens all the time. The trouble with us exceptionally moral people is that there are exceedingly few of us. We must partner up somehow, Kotler said, trying to lighten the mood.

—I don't believe it. If I were like you, I don't see how I could be with someone like me.

—But you aren't me. And I clearly haven't minded.

—I have always had my doubts about that. I have always wondered how you could be sincere. That compared to you, compared to Miriam, I was insufficient. And this has nothing to do with what they wrote about me in the newspapers. Believe me, they didn't write a single word that I couldn't have written myself.

—I think you have too dim a view of your own character.

—Do I? Not according to what I heard between you and Tankilevich. I heard what you said and I heard what he said. I'm not sure I would have behaved any differently in his place. So maybe I'm not who you thought I was.

—I see, Kotler said.

—He is a sick foolish old wreck of a man.

—And so should be absolved.

—Oh, I don't know, Baruch. Does it matter what I think, anyway? I'm in no position to say.

They looked at each other in silence and before Leora could turn away or Kotler offer something in reply, there came a cascade of notes that Kotler recognized as Leora's phone's ringtone. The notes, sampled from a vibraphone, bounced around the chamber of the cab. Leora let the phone ring a second time before she reached into her handbag. She let it ring a third and a fourth as she held it in her hand and read the display. And she gave Kotler a dubious glance before she touched the screen to accept the call.

—Hello, she said crisply.

Kotler tried to infer who might be on the other end. At present, a great many people could conceivably elicit from Leora such a response.

Yes, Kotler heard her say. Then, in the same tone, Yes, I know. And after a pause, looking directly at him, she said once more, Yes. She then took the phone from her ear and mutely extended it to him.

Kotler accepted it.

—Hello, he said and heard his daughter's voice in reply.

—I called first on your phone, Dafna said tightly. It didn't work.

Kotler felt for his own phone in his trouser pocket and tilted it away from the sun's glare. The screen was black. He pressed the button for the power but saw no change.

—The battery died, Kotler said.

—I was forced to call her.

—Then it must be important.

Through the handset Kotler heard a woman's voice over an intercom, resonating through the corridors of a public space. He couldn't decipher the words but he immediately assumed the worst. His heart and mind hurtled to the graveside, with the raw heaped earth, the shrieks and lamentations.

—You need to come home, Dafna said.

—I am coming home. I have a flight tonight. What happened?

—You talked to Benzion?

—Dafna, what is this? Are we playing some sort of game? Have you taken it into your head to discipline me? Tell me what happened.

—Benzion shot himself, she replied.

Kotler felt the impact as though the gun had just been fired and the bullet had struck him as well, its force concussing his chest.

—Did you hear me, Papa?

—Is he alive?

Leora had been following his conversation, and at this Kotler saw her body tense and her eyes grow wide and sharp with concern.

—Yes, Dafna said. He shot himself, but it was in the hand.

Kotler felt immediate, slavish relief, but also a rising sadness.

—He and two other soldiers. They all put their hands in front of Benzion's rifle and he fired. They called themselves the Brotherhood of the Right Hand. Benzion posted their declaration on his Facebook. A few lines from the Psalms. Now none of them will say a word.

—Where are you, Dafna?

—Hadassah Ein Kerem.

It was where Miriam had given birth to Benzion. The doctor had announced, *Mazal tov, Mr. Kotler, you have a son.* Kotler was invited to look at the child, the embodiment of so many of his dreams. He saw, almost to the exclusion of everything else, the infant's long, slender, finely wrought hands. On the little body, the hands seemed almost freakishly long, as if to mock Kotler's unspoken desire. For he'd secretly hoped that a child of his not be encumbered as he'd been. That the randomness of genes would, against probability, be kind to it. The sight of his son's beautiful hands filled him with pleasure and relief. He never ceased to admire them. He admired them too much, too effusively—his admiration, to his shame, carrying with it a taint of envy. How different his own life would have been if only he'd been granted such hands! In Benzion's act, Kotler discerned the deeper message intended for him: it was not by coincidence that his son had ruined the part of himself that his father loved best.

Now, in a hospital room, under military guard, his son was lying, while outside, before they were dispersed, the demonstrators would have assembled. Bearded and bedraggled supporters with their songs and banners. Through his window Benzion would hear their voices. *David, King of Israel, lives, lives and endures!*

—What did he say to you, Papa? Dafna asked.

—What did he say? He wanted my blessing, Dafna. To refuse orders.

—And what did you tell him?

—I told him I couldn't do that.

—Why?

—Because I disapproved, Dafna. I told him to find another way.

—Ha! Dafna derided him. Well, he found another way!

And what other way *had* Kotler imagined Benzion would find? Once the words were out of his mouth, did he follow the line of thought to the very end? He had. And had he been willing to accept that end? The graveside with the heaped earth? The sackcloth and ashes? No. But then why hadn't he said so unequivocally to Benzion? *My son, my dear one, anything but that!*

—You, Mama, Benzion: all of you with your sacred principles, Dafna said. And look at us. Look at all the good they have done us. Benzion wanted one word from you, Papa. Would it have killed you to give it to him? He is your son, not some enemy. Not the KGB or the prime minister. Well, now he gets to follow in your footsteps and go to jail, which should make you both happy.

A voice reverberated over the hospital intercom again and there was the sound of some commotion.

—This is pointless, she said. I have to go.

—How is your mother? Kotler interjected before she could hang up.

—In her element, Dafna said and ended the call.

SIXTEEN

At the next roadside stand, Kotler asked the driver to pull over.

Several folding tables were arrayed on the gravel turnout. On the tables dozens of clear glass jars glowed with different shades of honey, from palest yellow to deepest amber. On the ground, in wicker baskets, sprawled mounds of apricots and melons. And from metal racks flanking the tables, long strings of purple Yalta onions hung like curtains. Shaded under a large blue beach umbrella, a Russian woman and a Tatar boy in his teens sat on folding chairs. The boy was hunched over, doing something on his mobile phone, his thumbs moving in rapid patterns, while the woman gazed languidly at the highway and her approaching customers.

Kotler and Leora drew up to the table, though Kotler hardly looked at the offerings. He came to rest near the boy, who continued the compulsive thing he was doing with his phone. The woman fanned herself with her hand, though Kotler and Leora were the ones under the sun.

—Good day, the woman said.

—Good day, Kotler answered abstractedly, his thoughts else-where.

—Visiting Crimea?

—Visiting.

—Where from? she asked.

—Israel, Kotler answered plainly, since there was no longer any reason to dissemble.

—Ah, Israel, the woman said, investing the word with a completely arbitrary meaning.

A simple mercantile woman, without politics, Kotler thought. But that was all the consideration he was willing to give her. He asked Leora to borrow her phone—What for? she asked—Penance, he said—and took several steps away from the table. Only tangentially did he hear Leora's exchange with the woman.

—Yalta onions. Sweet as sugar. Taste.

—I believe you.

—Tell me, what do you know about honey?

—What everyone knows.

Kotler stood by the roadside. A truck plunged through the amplitude of dense air, and a wave of it washed over and staggered him. He had tried to do right, he thought, but had caused a great deal of hurt, even more than he'd expected. In some future of books and historians, he might yet be exonerated, but in the present he could not point to a single positive outcome. From the entire mess he would have liked to salvage at least one. There still remained a possibility, and in three or four phone calls he would know if it was feasible. He placed the first call to his office, for the number of a man he trusted at the JDC in

Jerusalem. From this man he received the address of the Simferopol Hesed, a phone number, and the name of its director, Nina
Semonovna Shreibman. He made his last call to her.

By noon they arrived at the Hesed. The driver, though he
claimed to know the city, had trouble locating the building.

—What kind of place is it? he asked.

—A Jewish center.

—They don't make it easy to find.

—Not by accident, Kotler said.

In the parking lot the driver took a space under the branches
of a juniper tree. The sun was high overhead and the air smelled
thickly of the surroundings, of the tar in the asphalt, the metal
and rubber of automobiles, the molten pitch of the trees.

—Keep track of your time, Kotler said to the driver. I don't
know how long we'll be. I hope not long.

—So long as you pay, it's all the same to me, the driver said,
lowered his window and reached for his newspaper. Reconciled
to waiting by vocation and heredity. A stern relentless life,
Kotler thought. Thus they'd sat in the trenches as the Panzers
advanced.

At the door to the Hesed, Kotler pressed the buzzer, and the
door clicked open to admit them. A man was seated behind a
desk in the vestibule. He looked to be in his fifties, with a long
melancholic face and graying hair. He regarded Kotler and Leora with no special interest.

—We're here to see Nina Semonovna.

—And you are?

—Baruch Kotler.

—One minute, the man said, Kotler's name evoking no more
recognition than had his face.

There was a telephone on his desk. The man lifted the receiver and dialed a number.

Kotler and Leora stood by. Kotler looked wryly at Leora as if to say: *And we feared I'd be recognized …*

A short exchange, and the guard hung up the phone.

—Go through, he said.

They went past the desk and into the narrow corridor, built along the Soviet administrative plan. In such corridors he had queued up for every piece of paper in his Soviet life, including, once upon a time, his exit visa. But here, instead, he saw a large wall map of Israel adorned with crayon drawings of camels, pomegranates, and menorahs. Beside it were the photographs of decorated Russian Jewish war veterans. This arrangement was also familiar. There had been a time when, in his capacity as an Israeli minister and an emancipated prisoner of conscience, he had visited many Jewish centers across the former Soviet Union. He'd done more of it in the years immediately after the Soviet Union's collapse, when he still possessed considerable stature and mystique. Back then it would have been unfathomable for a guard, for even a *charwoman,* to have failed to recognize him in the most far-flung Hesed. He had made those trips, his triumphant return, accompanied by reporters and photographers, and he'd posed and reminisced and delivered the same message to all of the Jews who'd come to lay eyes on him and clasp his hand: *Brothers and sisters, come home! Come to Israel!* And they had come. He didn't flatter himself that it was because of his personal invitation. The main credit went to Yeltsin and Kuchma and Lukashenko for providing such excellent reasons to leave. But it wasn't grandiosity for him to think he'd played a part. Even his worst enemies wouldn't quibble with that. He'd played a part and seen the results. Now here he was, doing what? Escaping those results? And what's more, taking the opposite line: telling a Jew to stay rather than go.

Not knowing which office was Nina Semonovna's, they walked the length of the corridor looking into the rooms. They saw the library—several shelves partially covered with books watched over by a woman who smiled meekly at them from behind a counter. Next, a nursery from which they could hear voices. Kotler saw three small children not yet able to walk and two others who were older. Various toys and games were scattered about the room. A young woman minded the littlest ones while a young man helped the older ones make cardboard shields emblazoned with drawings of intricate and colorful birds.

As they made their way along the corridor, Kotler noticed that they were being watched. A man, older than Kotler, stood at the double doors of one of the rooms and marked their progress. From a distance Kotler couldn't read the man's disposition. Nobody would have described him as menacing. He was a bald, slightly stooped, elderly Jew. Bifocals hung from a lanyard around his neck. But his expression, when they neared, was cagey.

—Good day, he said to Kotler, still inspecting him.

—Good day, Kotler replied.

—Have I seen you here before? the man asked.

—I've never been here before, Kotler said.

—You looked to me familiar, the man said.

—I have that kind of face.

—But you're Jewish?

—A popular question in Crimea.

This evasion the man disregarded, since his interest was in establishing the fact.

—But are you?

—I am, Kotler confirmed.

—*Redstu* Yiddish? the man inquired.

—A *bissel,* Kotler replied, to the man's great delight.

—Ah, *zeyer gut! Vos macht a yid?*

—A *yid dreitzikh,* Kotler said. *A Jew gets by,* his father's favored phrase.

—Come, the man said and indicated the room to his right. You must join us.

Kotler glanced inside. There was a proscenium at one end, an upright piano, and much empty floor space. In the middle of the room, a card table held a chessboard over which two men were bent. Three others sat near them but paid scant attention to the game. One gazed out at Kotler while the other two commiserated together in the language of commiseration.

—It is our Yiddish circle, the man announced. We meet every Sunday to talk in Yiddish.

—What you heard, I'm afraid, is the extent of my Yiddish. I'd be of no use to you.

—What about chess? We also play chess.

—My chess is worse than my Yiddish, Kotler said.

—No Yiddish and no chess? the man chided. What kind of Jew are you?

—The subject of much debate.

—And what about you? the man asked Leora. Maybe you have Yiddish? Young people are learning it now. Last year American students came with their professor to make a video interview with us.

—My Yiddish is worse than his, Leora said.

—And your chess?

—My chess is better.

—So join us. For old *kockers* like us, it will be nice to have such a lovely girl for company.

—I'm sorry, but not today, Leora said.

—If not today, then not tomorrow either, the man said without animus. But maybe with the coming of the *moshiach!*

—Then we will all play chess and talk Yiddish! Kotler said.

—May He come speedily and soon! the old man said.

He ducked back into the room to rejoin his circle, and Kotler and Leora were presented with one last door. Kotler knocked and a woman said, Come in.

The door opened onto an outer office containing two vacant desks with telephones and computers on them. A radio played at low volume, tuned to a Russian call-in program. The topic seemed to be the possibility of life on other planets. A scientific expert was speaking in favor.

Centered between the two desks was the door to the inner office. It was open. A woman sat behind a large desk and looked at Kotler. A cigarette smoked in an ashtray at her elbow. She picked up the cigarette and motioned for Kotler and Leora to enter.

—Have a seat, she said. And you may want to shut that door.

Kotler and Leora assumed two chairs in front of the desk.

—Do you object if I smoke? Nina Semonovna asked, holding her cigarette away from her face.

—No, Kotler said.

She rose and went to the window and pulled it partway open.

—It's hot outside and we have the air-conditioning, so I keep it closed. But this will release a little of the smoke.

She resumed her seat, deftly tapped the ash from her cigarette, and gave the indication that she was now ready to proceed. She was like other women Kotler had met who held similar offices. Disciplined, beleaguered, economical women with too many claims on their attentions. Unemotional but not unkind. Mothers of poor households, making due with not enough.

—So, Mr. Kotler, to what do I owe this honor? Nina Semonovna said with only the slightest trace of disingenuousness. You said very little on the telephone.

—Thank you for agreeing to see us on such short notice.

—It's not every day I get a call from Baruch Kotler. As I said, I consider it an honor. I hope I don't embarrass you by saying you were a hero to me.

—You embarrass me just enough. It's always nice to be remembered. Especially as one slips into obscurity.

—I doubt you are slipping into obscurity.

—It's not so terrible. The times change. Before, I could not have walked anonymously through a Hesed.

—You walked anonymously?

—Your guard didn't recognize me and a man in the corridor wanted to know if I was Jewish. It grounds the ego. Not a bad thing.

—The people are caught up in their problems.

—They have every right, Kotler said.

Nina Semonovna paused to bring the cigarette to her lips and looked from Kotler to Leora.

—My apologies, Kotler said. I failed to introduce you. This is Leora Rosenberg.

—I know, Nina Semonovna said. I read the papers.

—I see, Kotler said.

—So to the big mystery *Where did they go?,* the answer is *To Crimea.*

—Yes, Yalta. For reasons of childhood nostalgia. Ill placed.

—Why ill placed? Yalta, Crimea, are still beautiful. I see nothing wrong with this sort of nostalgia. I wish more Jews had it. We're not Odessa. We could do with the visitors.

—I agree. Crimea is beautiful. But it was not the right time for us to come. And things did not go as planned. A very strange coincidence befell us.

That was all he needed to say, Kotler saw, all the fragments he needed to provide for Nina Semonovna to assemble the picture. The mention of Yalta. Of a very strange coincidence. And now their appearance in her office. He watched her face go stony. Now he also understood: the queerness of her welcome had to do only with the scandal, what she had read in the papers. The connection to Tankilevich hadn't occurred to her yet.

SEVENTEEN

Tankilevich stood over the zinc tub in the yard. He had placed inside it the carbons of his letter to Chava Margolis. In his hand he held a box of matches. He would burn this letter. He had kept it this long because of a stupid self-deception. He'd imagined it would be discovered by his daughters after he died and that it would provide them with the truth about their enigmatic father. This had given him comfort. That which he could not bring himself to reveal to them in life, they could read in his own words after his death. But after his return from the pointless trip to the hospital, Tankilevich had been seized by the need to reread this letter, and he'd gone to the cabinet to get it. He hadn't looked at it in many years. He'd sent it ten years earlier, and it had been nearly that long since he had read it, though he believed he remembered with considerable accuracy what it contained.

After he reread it he went to find a matchbox.

Svetlana, meanwhile, had collapsed on the sofa. She lay there with a hand over her eyes. From this position she called after him—first imploring him not to go rummaging in the other room and then, when she saw him going back out to the yard, imploring him to stay in the house.

Reading the letter had brought back something that Tankilevich had managed to suppress. He had been right in that he remembered with a high degree of fidelity *what* he had written, but he had somehow forgotten *why* he had written it. And the reason for the letter, the purpose behind its composition, was shamefully manifest in its every line. He had written it soon after his brother's death. How could he have forgotten that? He had written it in a fit of financial desperation. This accounted for its pathetic, clamoring tone. Now he remembered. First he had begged Chava Margolis—*Forgive me, spare me, release me*—and, when she did not reply, he'd gone to beg Nina Semonovna. The letter was in the voice of a weakling, a man he despised. Not the man he wanted his daughters to discover. Instead, a man whose traces needed to be obliterated.

As he struck the match, he heard the telephone ring inside the house. For some reason, some intuition, he stood with the lit match in his fingers. The phone rang a second time before Svetlana answered it. Tankilevich continued to wait. He dropped the match onto the parched earth and stamped it out. Moments later, Svetlana came rushing out, holding the cordless telephone.

—For you, she said breathlessly.

Tankilevich took the phone and heard Nina Semonovna's voice. He heard her speak his name.

—Mr. Tankilevich, I have thought about our conversation.

—Yes, Tankilevich said.

—I have had a change of heart, Nina Semonovna said, though her voice gave no sign of it.

—Why? Tankilevich asked.

—Instead of asking questions, Mr. Tankilevich, I'd encourage you to say *Thank you.*

—I would like to know why, Tankilevich repeated.

—Why? Because the sun is in the sky, Nina Semonovna said. Tell me, would you prefer I reconsider?

Svetlana stood very close to Tankilevich and looked at him with horror.

Do as you please, Tankilevich thought. *Reconsider! Go to hell!*

—No, he said.

—I'll not wait for *Thank you,* Nina Semonovna said, adding, Your stipend will be mailed to you.

Tankilevich handed the receiver back to Svetlana.

—Well? she asked.

—Go and thank God, Tankilevich said.

He struck a match and put it to the letter.

EIGHTEEN

Between the domestic terminal of Kiev's Boryspil airport and the parking lot, there was a stand of mature chestnut trees, the bases of their trunks painted white. A few benches had been installed beneath them to create a little refuge. Leora told Kotler she wished to sit there before they went into the international terminal for the flight to Tel Aviv. It was past ten in the evening and the canopies of the trees corralled the darkness. A soft breeze blew. Leora and Kotler were not alone in the little refuge; others appeared to have gravitated there for the same reason: to skim a restful moment from a long journey. On one bench huddled a young family—the parents and two small children. One child was asleep in the father's arms, the other chewed sleepily on a bun given it by its mother. Sitting quietly by himself on another bench was a man, much obscured by the darkness, who sipped from a bottle of beer and smoked a cigarette. The silence was broken intermittently by the motor of a car starting in the parking lot and, every few minutes, by a plane lifting into the sky in a graceful line, soon visible only as a configuration of lights, pulsing and shining, white at the nose, the wings tipped green and red.

Leora and Kotler sat without speaking a small distance apart. After a time, Leora took her hand and placed it in Kotler's. Holding hands, they continued to sit without speaking. This was farewell with nothing to be said. Had they not come to Yalta, had they not met Tankilevich, had Benzion not shot himself, Leora wondered if the outcome for them would have been the same. If the train of events would have been any way unchanged. She thought of Benzion in the hospital with his mutilated hand. In her mind he was still very much a shy, serious, openhearted boy. She still felt a great deal of affection for him, and for Dafna and Miriam too. She had always felt privileged to be taken into their midst. But now she could not even think of paying Benzion a visit, sending him a card for his convalescence. She didn't doubt that his act had as much to do with the havoc in his family as the havoc in the land. Soon enough they would be returning to both, and she also to the ambiguity of what life held next. For this reason, she was glad to sit in the darkness and prolong their farewell, the purest, most intimate moment they would share on this trip. The rest of it was now clouded by a vague unpleasantness. She understood now what she should have understood all along. When Kotler refused the compromise on the park bench, it had sounded the death knell not for his marriage but for their affair. This trip, which they had entertained as a beginning, was always an ending. And, at root, her relationship with Kotler had been built upon a flawed premise. A girlish infatuation she had failed to banish. She had wanted her saint to also be a man. Which was like wanting day to also be night. A saint loved the world more than any single person, while a man loved one person more than the whole world. And so only a saint could live with a saint. She was no saint, though she had once aspired to be.

The thought of being not good enough for another person carried within it a condemnation of that person, and yet Leora felt it was a condemnation to which she alone was entitled. The rest of the world hadn't earned the right. And the rest of the world would resume for them as soon as they joined the line of people for the flight to Tel Aviv and lost their anonymity. They had already received a foretaste from Nina Semonovna. There had been the look on her face when she greeted them, but also the way she had treated Baruch when he asked for her help. This was what they could expect, and more.

—If it gets out, if there is trouble, Nina Semonovna had said, who will protect me? Are you any longer in a position to give assurances?

—Never mind assurances, Kotler said. Even at the best of times, there are no assurances. You do it not because of assurances but because it is right.

—Then I must not think it is right.

—You are punishing him needlessly. If I can forgive him, so can you.

Nina Semonovna then turned flintily to Leora.

—You have not said a word. Maybe we should also have your opinion?

Kotler turned to her as well.

—Let him live, she said.

Coda

On the flight to Tel Aviv, Kotler looked out from under the brim of his hat. He was in the middle seat; Leora had the window. A young Hasid with sidelocks and black garb sat on the aisle. The middle seat had originally been Leora's but the Hasid had politely asked if Kotler might be willing to switch with her. He hadn't explained why and they hadn't required him to. It was a small accommodation on a full plane. Not the place to make an egalitarian stand.

The airline was Ukrainian and the plane contained a mingling of humanity that now existed only on a flight like this. It was a little flying shtetl. A Sholem Aleichem story come to life. Sitting side by side, row by row, was every Jewish derivation. There were Hasids who worshipped God one way, rival Hasids who worshipped Him another, and the Zionist Orthodox who worshipped Him a third. There were the families of the merchant class who spoke Hebrew, and the families of the *biznismeni* who spoke Russian. There were the artists and intellectuals like Leora and Kotler, with their grand philosophical visions.

And there were the young American Jews, carefree, heedless, and a little dim, cushioned from history and entrusted with too much. Interspersed among them were Russians and Ukrainians, quiet and unperturbed, accustomed to these Jews from long-standing acquaintance. It was a model of coexistence as it may never have been and as it had failed to become. The moment the plane landed, it would dissolve, with everyone returning to his barricade.

How much changed, Kotler thought, was his outlook now compared to his first arrival in Israel. Practically antithetical. Twenty-five years earlier he had been filled with joy. The entire country had been astir. The prime minister had sent an official plane. They flew from Prague to Tel Aviv, just the Israeli aircrew, two diplomats, Miriam, and him. It was the high point of his life. He had never felt such promise, such optimism.

Now he was on an airplane surrounded by his people, his ideal little world, but he was hiding under his hat. He still retained his wonderment at the thought of Israel—that after millennia of exile, this country existed; that he'd had the good fortune to be born into this time; and that he had prevailed against an awesome foe to gain his place there—but he despaired for its future. His countrymen no longer waited impatiently for his arrival. Rather, he was the object of scorn and ridicule. His time had passed. The country desired a different kind of hero. Perhaps he should be proud, for he had supplied it with one.

But he remembered the night twenty-five years ago when he'd had his first glimpse of the land, the dark contours of Jerusalem scrolling by, the ancient city speckled with light, his heart stretched to the limit, as though pulled from above and below, his eyes welling with tears of primordial grief and thanksgiving, and the words of the Psalm resounding in his head in a strong mystical voice, *When the Lord brought back those that returned to Zion, we were like dreamers.* And he remembered the feel of Miriam's hand in his as they made their descent, holding her tight because otherwise he would burst from the plane from impatience, and the view of the tarmac with the honor guard and the brass band and the billowing flags, and the throng of a thousand jubilant faces, who were already singing when he stepped from the plane.

David, King of Israel, lives, lives and endures!

ACKNOWLEDGMENTS

The author wishes to thank the following people and organizations for their assistance:

Ben George at Little, Brown USA; Will Hammond at Viking/Penguin UK; Iris Tupholme at HarperCollins Canada.

Amanda Urban at ICM in New York; Margaret Halton at RCW in London; Daisy Meyrick at Curtis Brown UK. Thanks also to Ira Silverberg, who oversaw the book in its early stages.

Roman Chavdarov, for his exceptional generosity and hospitality in Crimea. My traveling companions, Michael Burns and Simon Shuster. Elana Kriulko and everyone I met at the Feodosia Hesed. Victoria Plotkina and everyone at the Simferopol Hesed—particularly Natalia Visotskaya, who has been a tremendous source of information about Crimean Jewry past and present. Большое вам спасибо.

Benny and Varda Shilo, for hosting me at the Weizmann Institute. Also at the Weizmann Institute: Amos and Galia Arieli, Shimon Levit, Rada Massarwa, and Tegest Aychek. At kibbutz Ein HaHoresh: Gadi, Ayala, and Itamar Marle; Yonat and Yossi Rotbein; and Elisha Porat. To the former refuseniks with whom I met in Israel: Yuli Kosharovsky, Hillel Butman, Evgeny Yakir, Alexander and Polina Paritzky. And, once again, to Enid Wurtman, for opening doors and much else. I'm also grateful to

Benny Begin, Hilik Bar, Yoram Meital, Talia Sasson, Boaz Katz, Meyer Shimony Bensimon, and Shlomo Azoulai for their time, as well as to Samer Makhlouf in Ramallah. Further thanks to Joel Braunold and OneVoice.

Many people at the American Joint Distribution Committee (JDC) were helpful to me at various stages of researching and writing the novel, among them Misha Mitsel, Gilla Brill, Mark Codron, Asher Ostrin, Ofer Glanz, and Michael Geller, who offered unflagging support.

Nell Freudenberger, Amity Gaige, and Larissa MacFarquhar read early drafts of the novel. Rabbi Martin Berman and Marilyn Berman also offered valuable advice.

Significant sections of the book were researched and written during fellowships at the Dorothy and Lewis B. Cullman Center for Scholars and Writers at the New York Public Library and at the Radcliffe Institute for Advanced Study at Harvard University. I am sincerely grateful to both organizations and to the colleagues I met there whose insights informed the novel, particularly those of Mortaza Mardiha.

And, as ever, I'm grateful to Hannah Young and Sara Bezmozgis.

ABOUT THE AUTHOR

David Bezmozgis is an award-winning writer and filmmaker whose fiction has appeared in *The New Yorker, Harper's, Zoetrope,* and *The Best American Short Stories.* He is the author of the story collection *Natasha* and the novel *The Free World,* and in 2010 he was named one of *The New Yorker*'s "20 Under 40" writers.